# LAST RITES

# THE MERCILESS IV

## LAST RITES

## DAN|ELLE VEGA

RAZORBILL®

## RAZORBILL®

An Imprint of Penguin Random House LLC
Penguin.com

RAZORBILL & colophon is a registered trademark of
Penguin Random House LLC.

## alloyentertainment

Produced by Alloy Entertainment
1325 Avenue of the Americas
New York, NY 10019

First published in the United States of America by Razorbill,
an imprint of Penguin Random House LLC, 2018

Copyright © 2018 Alloy Entertainment

Penguin Random House supports copyright. Copyright fuels creativity, encourages diverse
voices, promotes free speech, and creates a vibrant culture. Thank you for buying an
authorized edition of this book and for complying with copyright laws by not reproducing,
scanning, or distributing any part of it in any form without permission. You are supporting
writers and allowing Penguin Random House to continue to publish books for every reader.

LIBRARY OF CONGRESS CATALOGING-IN-PUBLICATION DATA
Names: Vega, Danielle, author.
Title: The merciless IV : last rites / by Danielle Vega.
Other titles: Last rites
Description: New York, NY : Razorbill, [2018]
Identifiers: LCCN 2018003871 (print) | LCCN 2018010488 (ebook) |
ISBN 9780448493510 (E-book) | ISBN 9780425292181 (hardback)
Subjects: | CYAC: Demoniac possession—Fiction. | Good and evil—Fiction. | Italy—Fiction. |
Horror stories.
Classification: LCC PZ7.1.V43 (ebook) | LCC PZ7.1.V43 Med 2018 (print) | DDC [Fic]—dc23
LC record available at https://lccn.loc.gov/2018003871ISBN 9780425292181

Printed in the United States of America

1 3 5 7 9 10 8 6 4 2

Design by Liz Dresner

This is a work of fiction. Names, characters, places, and incidents either are the product of the
author's imagination or are used fictitiously, and any resemblance to actual persons, living or
dead, businesses, companies, events, or locales is entirely coincidental.

# LAST RITES

To Terry *and* Becky
*and* Darla *and* Brad
*and* Bruce
(who gave me my first ever computer)

# CHAPTER 1

*Before*

It's been three weeks. That's twenty-one days. Five hundred and four hours. Thirty thousand, two hundred and forty minutes. I tried to break it down into seconds, too, but the numbers got too big and I couldn't do the multiplication in my head.

I'm woken up at seven every morning, when the night nurse delivers a bowl of cold oatmeal and warm OJ before heading to the front desk to clock out. It's always a different nurse, her face blandly sympathetic as she hands me the aluminum tray and plastic spoon. She (it's always a she) wears inappropriately cheerful scrubs. Laughing bananas. Puppies in sports gear. Teddy bears.

I eat alone in my dorm room, scraping the sides of the bowl to get every last bite. Not finishing your meal is considered a sign of passive aggression. Do it often enough and they make you talk about it in group therapy.

After breakfast we have art class—or what passes for art class in here. The nurses herd the girls sane enough to be trusted with scissors into the activity room, a low-ceilinged space with no windows and violently orange carpet. We sit in hard plastic chairs while the nurses pass out construction paper and Crayola crayons.

I select a blue crayon from the box and roll it between my fingers. It's half-melted, the paper long gone, and it leaves stains all over my hand.

I took an art class once. Figure drawing at the community college. My dad surprised me with a box of charcoal pencils and a ream of creamy white paper on my first day. I still remember how smooth and soft that paper was. How it soaked up the charcoal like it was thirsty.

I push the memory aside as I lift a piece of rough construction paper from the pile. Everything is rough here, in the institute. I doodle my name, Berkley, surrounded by daisies and hearts.

The girl sitting across from me is sniffing the red crayon. She pushes her hair back with one hand, revealing a face that's all eyes, and cheekbones like razorblades. She lowers the crayon to her mouth, sticks out her tongue—

"No, Cassandra." A nurse swoops down and plucks the crayon from between her fingers. "We don't eat the art supplies."

Cassandra looks like she's been denied a treat. She stares at me from across the table, running her tongue over cracked lips.

Lunch comes next. The line of girls stretches across the cafeteria and into the hall. We hold scratched aluminum trays and inch forward, staring into space like zombies.

The quiet bugs me—it has since I first got here. Lunch used to be the social event of my day. The cafeteria at my old school was a huge indoor courtyard. When you leaned back, you could see the windows from each floor of the four-story building, all the way up to the glass dome ceiling. Whom you sat with mattered, and people noticed if a boy stopped by your table to say hi or ask what you were doing that weekend.

Until I was a junior, I mostly existed outside of all that. My best friend, Tayla, and I were your typical wannabe girls. Maybe I'm not supposed to admit that, but it was true. We sat at the corner table in the cafeteria, watching the parade of boys circle Harper Cole and Mara O'Neal. I'd pretty much resigned myself to a boring high school existence until, one day, Harper leaned back in her chair and flicked a hand at Tayla and me as we made our way past her table.

"Hey, Berkley," she'd said, something mischievous flashing through her eyes as she jerked her chin toward the empty spot beside her. "Eat with us."

Five words and Tayla and I were in.

"Hurry up," the lunch lady shouts at me. Her voice snaps me out of the memory and back to the cold, gray institute cafeteria. I'm next in line. I slide my lunch tray forward, looking around for someone to sit with.

There's Bridget, who thinks the rats that live inside the walls talk to her. Or Amelia, who says her mother's death was a conspiracy covered up by the United States government. Or Lauren, who . . .

Whatever. You get it.

I take my tray to an empty table in the corner and sit down. I wonder what Mara and Harper are doing at this very second. I picture Harper lounging on the floor of her NYU dorm, impatiently flicking through some fashion magazine she buys only for the perfume samples, waiting for spring break to start. And Mara will be crouched over her tiny little desk just down the hall, covering a giant textbook in Post-it notes and studying for midterms. She was our high school valedictorian, but she has to get straight As to keep her scholarship—not that she needs it. Her parents are loaded.

I stir my serving of mystery meat with a plastic spoon. I wonder if Harper and Mara are thinking of me, too. If they're picturing me in here.

God, I hope not.

After lunch, I head back to my room. I hear voices and swearing outside the thin walls. Sounds like another fight in the common room, probably over whether to watch reruns of *Keeping Up with the Kardashians* or *The Big Bang Theory*, which are somehow the only two television programs that ever play on the bolted-down television. The shouts rise, and then cut off abruptly. One of the nurses must've threatened medication.

Technically it's my free hour, which means I could be arguing in the common room, too, or at least wandering through the vomit-colored halls, getting some exercise. Instead, I collapse on my cot. I punch my lumpy pillow into a shape vaguely resembling an old rock and wedge it beneath my back, where it immediately deflates.

I sneak the bottle of Wite-Out from under my mattress and drag the spongy brush over my nails in long, even strokes. I used to love painting my nails. I'd find nail-art pics on Instagram, watch tutorial after tutorial until I could perfect the tiny field of polka dots, draw a perfect sunflower using a toothpick and a cotton swab. Tayla wanted me to teach her, but her hands always shook.

The nurses took all my polish when I checked in. Apparently some of the girls in this place actually drink the stuff. I nabbed the Wite-Out from the reception desk when they weren't looking.

A girl screams. The sound is high and shrill, and it echoes through the hallways outside my room. My muscles are like rubber bands, snapping tight. I focus on the white streaks of paint sliding across my nails so I don't have to think about how the scream doesn't sound human. It sounds like a dying animal, a fox or a cat.

The door to my room opens with a creak of rusty hinges, and a girl I don't recognize walks past my bed.

"Cool nails," she says, nodding at my hand. She's Latina, with long, dark hair, brown eyes, and brown skin. "They're sort of mod, right? Very 1960s London."

I pop an eyebrow at her. She doesn't look like she eats crayons or talks to rats, but you can't always see a girl's crazy. She flops onto the bunk across from me—which I'd been using as an open-air closet for the two additional blue, nondescript T-shirts and drawstring pants I'm allowed—and kicks her paper-thin slippers to the floor.

"Uh, thanks?" I push up to my knees, careful not to screw up my nails. "But who're—"

A nurse appears at the doorway, clipboard in hand. "Berkley Hubbard, meet Sofia Flores," she says, not bothering to look up from her papers. "Your new roommate."

Sofia jerks her chin at me by way of greeting. I'm still processing and can't form words. I thought I had a private room.

The nurse doesn't wait for my response. "Sofia, is there anything else I can get you before I go?"

"Cigarette?" Sofia deadpans.

We don't get a lot of attempts at humor in here, and I don't know if I'm more surprised by the bad joke or by the fact that the nurse actually laughs, her stomach heaving beneath kitten-print scrubs.

"You're a hoot, darling," she says, still chuckling as she starts to pull the door shut. "I'll leave the two of you to get acquainted."

And then she's gone. Sofia leans against the wall, crossing her legs beneath her. "So," she says, eyes following the exposed pipe stretching across our ceiling. "What're you in for?"

Anywhere else this might seem like the kind of question you don't touch until you get to know each other. In here, it's the equivalent of asking what college you go to or what you're majoring in. It comes right after "Hey, what's your name?"

"I had a breakdown . . . thing," I say, trying for casual. "I lost it at my first college party. I'm told there was a lot of screaming and that I sort of pulled a knife on some guy."

Sofia's eyebrows go up. "You're *told?*"

"Yeah, well, I was pretty stoned. Don't remember much. My parents totally overreacted, sending me here." A jerk of my shoulder like it's no big deal. I turn back to my nails and, muttering, add, "After what happened to Tayla, it's not like they were going to take any chances."

"Who's Tayla?"

Thinking about her sends heat climbing up my neck. I pick at a chunky glob of Wite-Out near my thumb. "She was my best friend my whole life, but she committed suicide last year. I had the panic attack a few months later." I clear my throat. "You?"

Sofia says, without missing a beat, "Murder."

I look up too quickly and search her face to see if she's serious. She stares back at me with eyes so empty she could be a doll.

Then her lips split into a grin. "Come on, I'm kidding."

"*Oh.*" I laugh—nervously at first, and then for real. Laughing feels good. *Really* good. It's weird how much you miss the little things. "Jerk."

"I was in solitary for a month after a little disagreement with some visitors, but they've finally deemed me sane enough to enter the wider population of crazies." Sofia flips her hair over one shoulder and starts to braid her thick curls. "Lucky me, right?"

"Why solitary?" I'm not sure if this is cool to ask, but Sofia rolls her eyes like she couldn't care less.

"Suicide risk. At least that's what it says on my forms."

"Oh." I don't know what to say to that so I squirm, pretending I'm trying to get comfortable in my makeshift nest of threadbare blankets and scratchy sheets. "I'm sorry."

"Don't be, I'm fine."

She seems fine, at least more "fine" than anyone else in this place. I study her face for a moment, trying to figure out what kind of girl she was before. She's pretty. It's not flashy pretty, so you don't notice it right away, but she's got big eyes and long lashes and full, heart-shaped lips. I bet she was popular.

Her fingers are still working at her hair, and I notice she has a tattoo in the crook of her hand: a serpent with a long, pornographic tongue, a headdress made of feathers propped on its scaly head. It's an old-school, punk-rock tattoo. Homemade, the lines all sketchy and blue. My dad used to have a coffee-table book filled with prison tattoos. I think he liked the way it contrasted with our Connecticut-chic décor.

"Is that real?" I ask, eyebrows lifting.

Sofia tilts her hand to the side, frowning at the tattoo like she just remembered it was there. "This thing? As real as it gets."

I scoot to the edge of my bed. "Did you do it yourself?"

"I used to be friends with this chick who worked in a tattoo parlor. She showed me how to do it using just a needle and ink. It's impossible to find enough toilet paper in this place, but they've got needles and ink *everywhere*."

"You did it in here?"

"Yep. In solitary."

I imagine her crouched on the floor in solitary, stabbing her hand over and over, smearing ink into the bleeding wound. I have to bite the inside of my cheek to keep my lip from curling. "Sounds like it hurt."

A shrug. "That's kind of the point, isn't it? They put us through so much shit in this place. I want to walk away with something to show for it."

That's the polar opposite of what I want. I want to walk away from this place without a mark. I want it to be like I was never here in the first place, like this was all some crazy nightmare.

Lately, that seems impossible. I'm half-convinced the smell of this place is seeping into my skin. That I'll never be able to scrub off the stink.

"You'll change your mind," Sofia says, like she knows exactly what I'm thinking. I look up with just my eyes, suddenly wary.

"What do you mean?"

"You're thinking that you don't want anyone to know you had to come to a place like this, right?" I don't believe in mind-reading psychic nonsense. But this is spooky.

Sofia leans forward, hands curling around her bed's metal frame. "But you'll change your mind. You went through hell and survived to tell the tale. A couple more weeks of this shit and you'll want to wear it like a badge of honor."

"I don't know about that." But my voice doesn't sound sure, even to me.

Sofia studies me for another moment, dark eyes moving over my face. Finally, she leans back, mattress springs screeching as she recrosses her legs and lets her head drop against the wall. "You're probably right. What the hell do I know? You seem like a good girl. Not like the other fuckers here."

She says *good girl* like it's a compliment, but I just met her so I can't be sure.

"I bet you only have a couple more weeks left," she adds. Her eyes flick over my face, narrowing. "Am I right?"

"Three," I admit. "I'm already counting down the seconds. You?"

She presses her lips together, eyes moving to the door and then back to me again. "Are you kidding? They're never letting me out."

I can't tell whether she's serious. I attempt a smile, waiting for her to crack up again and tell me she's only kidding. But she doesn't say a word. Just stares back at me with those strange, empty eyes.

The girl in the TV room starts screaming again. Short, staccato bursts this time, the sounds rising and falling like hammer blows. My shoulders go rigid as I wait for her to stop. I glance at the door, one hand going to my throat. I can feel the *bomp bomp bomp* of my heartbeat in my fingertips.

The screaming goes on and on.

# CHAPTER 2

## *After*

My packed suitcase sits on the bed in front of me, filled to the brim with sundresses and strappy sandals, cropped tank tops and plastic sunglasses. Mara, in typical detail-oriented Mara fashion, made sure I knew the exact weather forecast when we Skyped last night so I could pack appropriately for the insane heat. I could see the sweat dotting her pale forehead, her white-blond pixie-cut hair stuck to her skin.

I close my eyes and imagine the same warmth sliding over my skin. The AC at the institute was always turned too high. Even now—seven months after my release—I can still remember that bone-deep cold. It used to wake me in the middle of the night, shivering so badly my jaw ached.

I pull my cell out of the back pocket of my jean shorts. A notification has popped up, alerting me that my flight is on time and will depart in two hours and forty-five minutes. I shimmy my shoulders in excitement.

*Finally*, I think, sliding my phone back into my pocket. Time to go. There are still two weeks left in July, and I'm planning to live it up with my two best friends in Italy. Mara and Harper have been there all summer, doing an arts program, and I'm finally able to join them. I yank my suitcase off the bed, grab my tote bag from the back of my bedroom door, and hurry down the stairs. *Dolce vita!*

My parents wait for me at the front door. I offered to get an Uber, but "Dan Hubbard won't let any daughter of his head to the airport alone!" (My dad actually said this while clapping me on the shoulder—God, *so* embarrassing.) He took the morning off so he could drive me to Bradley International, but Mom couldn't get anyone to cover her morning classes, so she's seeing me off here.

It would've been easier if we'd said goodbye last night. I can practically feel the nerves vibrating off Mom's skin.

"Are you sure you're ready for this?" Her hands are at her neck, sliding her pearl necklace through her fingers. She pinches each pearl, counting them like they're rosary beads. "Daddy and I have been talking, and it's just that Italy is so far away . . ."

"Don't worry, I told her you can handle it," Dad adds, throwing me a wink. He puts a hand over Mom's to keep her from rubbing the finish off her pearls.

"You're sure it's not too soon?" Mom asks. We look alike—same long auburn hair, round face, and full mouth—but now her lips are pulled tight over her teeth, making her look older than she is. The minuscule lines on her forehead are out in full force.

"I promise, I'll be fine." I lean in, planting a kiss on her cheek. "Mara and Harper will be with me the whole time, and I know not to push myself if I start feeling out of it."

Those are her words. She's repeated the phrase about a million times over the last week. *Just don't push yourself* . . . And that's when she's not watching me like a hawk. Monitoring my eating. Making sure I don't sleep too late. Casually checking what I'm reading, just to make sure it's not something too "upsetting."

I swear, last week she was about to psychoanalyze some dumb dream I had about a missing rabbit, but Dad stopped her before she could get the words out. Thank God.

"Well . . ." Mom still looks unsure. "Just promise to call."

"Of course."

She wraps her arms around me before I can pull away, hugging me firmly. She's too thin—I can tell she hasn't been eating since I got back—and her spine digs into my fingers, each bone a sharp point. "Be safe."

I give her a tight squeeze before wiggling out of her grip, waving over my shoulder as I head for the door.

I step outside, and the weight of her worry falls from my shoulders, like a discarded sweater. The sun is warm on my bare legs, reminding me that, before long, I'll have Italian sun and Italian streets and Italian *boys* to keep me company.

I tip my head back, inhaling deeply. The sky is achingly blue. I want to drink it in, hold it inside me. My luck is finally changing. It's been seven long months since I left the institute behind, and, still, *this* feels like my first real moment of freedom.

*Italia*, here I come.

The Italian heat hits me like a wall.

The airport doors whoosh closed behind me, taking all the manufactured cold air with them. I scoop the hair off the back of my neck with one hand, gasping. My legs and underarms have already gone sticky, and I'm starting to feel a little jet-lagged. Eight hours cramped in coach will do that, I suppose. A dull headache pounds through my skull.

I grab my suitcase and start wheeling toward the curb, eyes peeled for a taxi, when light brown curls and a blond pixie cut catch my eye.

I release a shocked laugh. "Harper? Mara?"

Their heads swivel around.

"Berkley!" Harper squeals. She's wearing oversized Audrey Hepburn in *Roman Holiday*–style sunglasses that cover half her face, and a dazzling smile unfolds beneath them. "We thought you'd *never* get here."

I drop my suitcase and pull Harper into a hug. "I can't believe you came all the way out to the airport to pick me up!"

"Of course we did," Mara says, fanning herself. She's somehow managed to keep her skin pale as porcelain despite the torturous Italian sunshine. "What are friends for?"

"You guys are the best." I move in to hug her next. She seems to stiffen as I wrap my arms around her shoulders, but when I let her go she tucks a lock of white-blond hair behind her ears, smiling, and I figure I imagined the pause of awkwardness.

"How was your trip?" Mara asks. "We were *so* worried when your flight got delayed."

"Were you?" The plane was held on the runway for about an hour before takeoff, but after that everything was fine. "It really wasn't a big deal."

"Are you kidding? We were practically *yelling* at the

woman at the information desk, but it's like she didn't even care." Harper rolls her eyes dramatically. "Italians *hate* giving a straight answer to anything, you'll see. She kept being like, *Maybe it'll land in the next twenty minutes? Maybe it'll be tomorrow? Who knows?*"

I laugh, sure that they're joking. They both smile back, but Harper can't stop tapping her foot, and Mara keeps winding and unwinding her fingers. They were actually worried.

I clear my throat. "Well, I hope you didn't have to wait for long . . ."

Harper waves my apology away with a flick of her hand. "Oh! It was *totally* fine. Don't worry about it."

"We just didn't want you to be freaked," Mara adds. "Those airplane seats can be so claustrophobic . . . Anyway, you're going to love it here. The students in our program are really *so* nice."

"You'll meet them all at dinner tomorrow night." Harper's eyes go to my suitcase. "Is that all you packed?"

I'd been so proud of myself for getting all my clothes into a single carry-on, but now the bag seems comically small, especially for two weeks in a foreign country. "Should I have brought more?"

Mara shakes her head. "No, no—don't worry about it. Harper brought her entire closet, obviously, but I packed light, too. You'll be fine."

"I just like *options*," Harper says, adjusting her sunglasses. "I'm competing with Italian women here. I need to make sure I look my best at the clubs."

"Although, we obviously don't have to go out clubbing if you don't want to," Mara cuts in. "It's no big deal!" I frown—I like going out just as much as they do—but Harper takes my suitcase before I can respond and starts pulling it down the sidewalk.

"Oh, right, of course not," she adds. "Mara and I've been dancing practically every night this week, so it's probably time for a break."

"She's such a bad influence," Mara says. "I've barely gotten any studying done the entire trip."

Harper rolls her eyes. "We're in *Italy*."

"And I'm premed. I can't just take two months off." Mara turns back to me. "We can just take it easy tonight—dinner and wine back at the apartment." She glances at Harper. "I mean, neither of us can show our faces at Galleria anytime soon."

Harper bursts out laughing. "Oh my God! I still can't believe the bartender *said* that to you . . ."

"I'm pretty sure I could see his nipples through that tank top."

"So gross! Did you—"

"We don't have to stay in because of me," I cut in. "I brought plenty of stuff to wear. Going out could be fun!"

"If you want. But seriously, we don't have to do any-thing you're not comfortable with." Mara lifts her arm to wave down the zippy white taxi that just rounded the corner. "We're happy to do something low-key. No big deal."

It's the second time she's said *no big deal* in the last five minutes. It feels like something they talked about before I got here. *If Berkley gets weird, just act like it's no big deal. Pretend everything's normal.*

Which means they think I'm still sick. They're wor-ried they'll be the ones who have to clean up after me when I lose it.

The taxi skids to a stop. Harper leans through the front window, saying something in Italian. Mara loads my suitcase into the trunk and climbs into the backseat. I slide in beside her, and she grabs my hand.

"We're going to have so much fun," she says, squeez-ing my fingers.

Harper sits next to me, pulling the door shut. "Oh my *God*, I can't wait for you to see the apartment. It's to *die* for."

"The place is insane," Mara adds in an undertone. "You know how Harper loves a little drama? Well, she went a little overboard when she picked this place."

"I can't wait," I say, relaxing. At least this feels like it's supposed to. The three of us packed into the back of a taxi, giggling. This is what I'd been picturing all those months stuck in Connecticut, and it's so right that I have to bite back a smile. My friends came all this way to greet me at the airport, after all. They didn't have to do that.

It's about an hour's drive from the airport to the village. The taxi takes us down a wide road lined with dying sunflowers and cypress trees. Earlier in the year, the fields were probably beautiful, filled with bursts of yellow, but by now the unrelenting sun has turned most of the flowers brown, leaving miles of packed dirt and rocks where the plants have all died. The sky above the field is dotted with black.

"Something must've died," Mara mutters, and I realize the black dots are crows. Hundreds of them. They get closer, wings outstretched as they land on a spot far off in the field. "That's the only reason crows act like that."

"Thank you, professor." Harper pulls a compact out of her bag to check her makeup.

I lean partway across Harper's lap to get a better look. But there are too many crows to see anything else in the field. They swarm together, wings overlapping wings, pointed beaks pecking at something just out of view.

And then the taxi zooms past, and I watch them grow smaller and smaller in the rearview mirror.

# CHAPTER 3

The cab makes a sharp turn onto a cobblestone road, and Cambria appears, like a mirage. It's a smaller town than I expected, all narrow streets and quaint squares and centuries-old towers. The crumbling stone village seems to rise out of the olive groves and wheat fields. Weeds grow out of windows and climb up walls. Everything is heavily coated in layers of dirt.

A cow with visibly protruding ribs stumbles, lazily, into the middle of the road, and the cabbie skids to a stop. He lays on the horn, swearing in Italian until the creature casts us a withering glance.

"The village is overrun with livestock," Harper explains, wrinkling her nose. "It's so gross."

I watch the cow lazily trot away. "I don't know. You don't think they're kind of sweet?"

"Say that after some wandering cow stops your taxi for the *fortieth* time," Mara says, and Harper snickers.

One hairpin turn later and the cab skids to a stop in front of what appears to be an old church. The exterior is all stone arches and dirty stained-glass windows. A gargoyle leans over the double doors, staring down at our cab with wide, unblinking eyes.

Mara starts digging around for euros, while Harper and the cabdriver exchange pleasantries in Italian. I should offer to pay. I reach for my tote—

"We got this," Harper says, waving my hand away.

I hesitate. "Really?"

"Definitely. Don't even worry about it."

It feels weird to let her pay, but I tell myself I'll buy wine later to make up for it.

I swing my bag over my shoulder and dart across the street as the taxi peels away in a cloud of exhaust. It doesn't occur to me that we're headed for the church until Harper stops in front of the massive doors, a set of heavy keys dangling from her fingers.

I have to fight to keep my mouth from dropping open. "*This* is where we're staying?"

"I know. Isn't it amazing?" Harper pushes the door open with a grunt. "And it's only, like, fifty euros a night. Crazy, right?"

"A ton of students got their own places," Mara explains. "CART dorms are tiny."

"And what's the point of coming to Italy if you aren't going to live among Italians?" Harper adds.

"Definitely," I say. Cambria Art Institute's summer program—or CART—is the reason they're here. But it doesn't sound like they've been going to many classes. Dinner with their professor tomorrow night is the first I've heard of an actual teacher.

"We're pretty sure someone got murdered here and that's the only reason we're getting such a good deal," Mara's saying. She takes my suitcase from me and wheels it inside.

There are bikes and tennis shoes piled by the front door and a row of metal mailboxes hanging from the wall, crumpled envelopes overflowing from the cubbies. The heavy door swings shut behind us, making the floor tremble beneath my feet. It's at least ten degrees colder in here, and the walls are so thick that they block sound completely.

We climb three flights of cracked stairs and end up in front of a doorway that's a perfect miniature of the main entrance. A tiny gargoyle peers over the top of the stone arch as Harper fumbles with her keys.

"You ready?" she asks, but she throws the door open and herds me inside before I answer. The door slams shut behind us, and I'm entirely surrounded by walls painted a deep, bloody red.

"Looks like it was decorated by Dracula, doesn't it?" Mara says, ushering me into the living room. She leans my suitcase near a leather settee and switches on a floor lamp. The sudden light makes me squint.

Velvet curtains cover the windows, blocking the setting sun. The furniture is all heavy and dark, with ornate carvings cut into the wood and elaborate images stitched into the fabric.

"Want the tour?" Harper claps her hands together, giddy.

I grin at her excitement, shoving my hands into my back pockets. "Lead the way."

We check out her room first. It looks a lot like the living room—the same dark wood and heavy fabrics—but a four-poster bed sits against the middle of the wall, directly across from a wide balcony overlooking the entire city of Cambria. Clothes and shoes are strewn over every surface.

"You didn't lie about bringing your whole closet," I say.

"When in Rome—well, sort of," Harper explains, pushing the balcony door open. A gasp of warm air sweeps into the room, carrying the comforting smell of bread and the sound of a woman below arguing with someone in Italian. "We drink espresso out here every morning. You'll see."

Mara's room is up next. It's not as big as Harper's, and there's no four-poster, but a fluffy white duvet covers her bed, and the Juliet balcony overlooks a massive field of sunflowers. Thick stacks of books crowd the walls, but the thin layer of dust on their covers tells me they haven't been opened in weeks.

"Whoa," I breathe, impressed. The setting sun has turned the field gold and fiery.

"I know," Mara says from behind me. She casts a guilty look at her books. "You can see why studying hasn't been at the top of my agenda."

My room is through the last door at the end of a long, narrow hall. I try not to look disappointed when Harper pushes the door open and flips on the light, but compared to the other two bedrooms, mine looks more like a closet. A narrow bed slouches against the far wall, and there's a heavy wardrobe shoved into the corner. A fresco painting hangs above the bed, the sky filled with some gruesome battle scene between angels and devils while, on the ground below, all the humans scream in agony. A single girl has been tied to a stake, fire curling at her toes.

There's a tiny plaque at the bottom of the painting. I lean closer to read it: *Il Sacrificio di Lucia*.

"That's a famous story from Cambria's history," Harper explains. "Legend has it that the whole town went totally mental in the sixteenth century . . ."

"Nice, Harper," Mara says, shaking her head. To me, she adds, "The town was sinning too much, according to historians. God punished them by causing a drought, keeping the crops from growing, that sort of thing."

"That's basically what I *said*," Harper mutters.

"The town sacrificed Lucia as a penance, and they all lived happily ever after," Mara finishes. "Cool story, right?"

"Charming." I'm too focused on the extreme tininess of my room to listen to the story, and I guess a little bitterness slips into my voice. Mara and Harper share a look.

"We know it's small," Harper says apologetically.

"It's just that we've been here all summer, so it made sense for us to take the bigger rooms," Mara adds.

Suddenly I feel like a complete jerk. I *wanted* to come here, didn't I? It's not their fault there are only two good rooms. "It's perfect, guys, really. Don't worry about it."

I plop down on the bed, determined to love my tiny room. It might be small, but the ceiling soars above me, and sure, there's no balcony, but there *is* a flower box below the window. The flowers are all sort of dead, but still.

I squint at the flower box, spotting movement. A black cat waits outside, pawing at the glass.

"Ooh, now you get to meet Lucky." Mara unlatches the window and pushes it open so the cat can slip inside. It rubs the length of its body against Mara's arm and then leaps to the floor, vanishing beneath my bed. "He's a stray, but we feed him, so sometimes he comes and hangs out here. He likes to sit on my feet while I read."

"He also likes chewing up expensive leather handbags," Harper mutters, glaring at Lucky. "Which is why he's no longer allowed in *my* room."

"He's so cute." I scoot to the edge of the bed and lean over, spotting two yellow eyes in the darkness. I reach out a hand. "C'mere, Lucky."

"We should let you get settled in," Harper says. I'm still upside down, so I can't see her, but the sound of her voice tells me she's hovering near the door. "You must be exhausted, what with jet lag and everything. You want to take a nap?"

I flip my head up, pushing my hair back with one hand. I wasn't planning on sleeping, but now that she's mentioned it, my eyes do feel a little heavy. I swallow a yawn. "Maybe a short one?"

"Totally," Mara says, and pulls my door shut. Their footsteps thump down the hallway.

Lucky races out from beneath the bed and leaps up

next to me. A second later, he's curled himself into a ball on my pillow, purring.

I don't know how long I sleep, but I wake to the sound of giggling.

I groan and lift a hand to my face, blinking. The light seeping in from beneath the curtains is no longer gold and dusty—now it's a deep, hazy blue. I frown and push myself up to my elbows, upsetting Lucky. He meows, lazily, and hops off the bed.

The giggling outside my door gets louder.

"Oh my God, you're so *bad*!" Mara squeals.

Then Harper: "Shh . . . you'll wake her up."

*What the hell?* I climb out of bed and creep across the room, easing my bedroom door open a crack.

Mara and Harper hover near the front door. They've changed clothes: Mara's in a strappy black top over cutoff jeans, wobbling a bit on towering high heels that she's obviously borrowed from Harper's closet, while Harper wears a gauzy white sundress with brown sandals laced around her ankles. She's got her purse balanced on her hip, and she's rooting around inside for something.

"Hurry!" Mara whispers, giggling into a fist. "We don't want to—" She lifts her head, eyes meeting mine, and her pale face goes a shade lighter than it is already. *"Shit."*

Lucky slips between my feet as I step into the hallway, still rubbing the last of the sleep from my eyes. "What's going on?"

Harper pulls her hand out of her purse, fingers clutching the heavy set of keys. "We didn't know when you'd wake up."

"You've been napping for hours," Mara adds, studying her fingernails.

I try to ignore the hurt building in my chest. "So you were just going to leave without me?"

"No!" Harper says, too quickly. She and Mara exchange a look. "It's just . . . a bunch of people from CART are at the trattoria down the street. We were going to go hang with them until you woke up."

"We figured you might want to sleep for a while," Mara says.

"We left a note," Harper finishes, lamely.

I don't believe they actually left a note. In fact, I don't believe anything they just said. They've been acting weird since I got here, and I'm about a million percent certain they were going to ditch me tonight.

I don't look half as cute as they do, in my plane-rumpled clothes, my face still red and puffy from my nap, but I'll be damned if I let them leave without me. I snatch my tote bag from the back of the door. "I'm up now. Let's go."

Harper and Mara's CART friends take up an entire table in the back of the tavern. They seem cool enough. They all smile and say *hey* when Harper introduces me, but their faces blur together, and I quickly lose track of their names—they're all called Emma or Emmy or Emilia.

Mara immediately gets drawn into a discussion about the relationship between two modern artists I've never heard of before. I try to follow along, but I know nothing about Italy or art or anything else they're talking about. I turn to Harper, hoping she'll talk to me, but she's admiring some girl's new leather shoes and seems to have forgotten that I'm there.

Finally I lean across the table, taking advantage of a break in the conversation. "Should I grab the first round?"

Harper gives me a thumbs-up without looking up from the shoes. I don't think Mara hears me.

I take my time heading across the trattoria. This isn't what I'd been expecting. I kind of figured things would be weird—the three of us haven't had a chance to hang out since I got back from the institute—but I didn't think they'd be *this* weird. Harper and Mara have been nice enough, I guess. But there's something beneath the smiles, something that makes me wonder if they want me here at all.

I slide my elbows onto the sticky bar and wave over the bartender. "Um, three—whoops, I mean *tre*—uh, shots of"—I point to a bottle filled with vibrant green liquid—"whatever that is. *Grazie.*"

The bartender pulls the bottle down from a wooden shelf and pours three shots. She jerks her chin at the CART students.

"You're with them?" she asks in perfect English, the barest trace of an Italian accent curling her r's.

"No, I'm not in the program. Just visiting for two weeks."

"Ah." She smiles, showing off a mouthful of perfectly straight, white teeth. She's a classic, curvy Italian beauty with wicked eyes and thick, dark hair that she wears in a short shag. It's dark in here, but I think I see green strands just behind her ears. She pushes the shots toward me. "Did you just get in?"

I fiddle with the wad of euros I just pulled out of my purse. "Is it that obvious?"

"A tiny bit." The bartender flicks a hand at my money, laughing. She has tiny tattoos around her hand: horseshoes and stars. They remind me of Lucky Charms. "The first round is on the house. Welcome to Italia."

I thank her and curl my hands around the shots, taking them back over to Mara and Harper. I squeeze in at the end of the table and set the shot glasses down, sending a drop sloshing over my fingers.

"Ooh, shots!" Harper says, eyes lighting up.

Mara raises her eyebrows. "That was sweet of you."

"In honor of my first night," I explain, handing them out. I lift a glass: "To the best trip of our lives."

The three of us clink our shot glasses together and drink. Mara and Harper cringe and crumple their faces, like they've never had alcohol before, but I don't mind the taste of the liquor. In fact, I hold it on my tongue for a second longer than necessary, relishing the burn.

I look around just as a crowd of Italians enter the trattoria, talking and laughing.

"Ooh, the tour guides have arrived," Harper says, wiggling her eyebrows. "The Demons' Walk tour ends right next door, so they all end up partying here after freaking out tourists with stories of human sacrifice."

"Harpy, look, it's our favorite," Mara says, pointing. Harper giggles as Mara nudges my shoulder. "See, right over there? He doesn't come every night. Dreamy, right?"

I turn. A guy stands near the door, and at first, I think there's no way he's worth drooling over. He's facing away from me, but he looks pretty nondescript. Tall and thin, with dark hair and tanned skin, just like every other Italian in this town.

Someone calls his name—*Giovanni*—and he turns, smiling. His hair is a little curly in the front, and his nose is long and straight in a way that reminds me of old pictures of Roman emperors. Black stubble shades his jaw and cheeks, and I can see the fan of his dark eyelashes from all the way across the room.

I swallow and turn back around, revising my initial opinion. *Dreamy* suddenly seems too soft a word for the tall, dark tour guide. He looks like he stepped out of a painting.

"He's the best guide in town," Mara is saying, "and not just because he's gorgeous. He's really smart, too. I've already done the Demons' Walk tour twice."

Harper laughs. "Yeah, Mara, you did the walk twice because he's *smart*."

I turn, catching another glimpse of Giovanni leaning over the bar. He pushes his shirtsleeves up to his elbows, revealing tanned skin and lean muscle. The bartender with the green strips dyed into her hair says something, and Giovanni laughs, the sound rising over the rest of the tavern's noise. I feel a small twinge of jealousy. They look right together, beautiful and hip.

Then, out of nowhere, Giovanni turns, shifting his gaze toward the back of the room. For just a second, I think he's looking right at me. But then his dark eyes flicker away.

People keep filing into the trattoria until, eventually, the conversation gets drowned out by the crush of other voices. Someone turns up the music. European techno. It's weird, close enough to music I've heard before to feel familiar, but just *off* enough to sound foreign. I close my eyes and start to sway. The music is all bass. I feel it vibrating in my bones.

"Let's dance." I stand, reaching for Harper's hands. She weaves her fingers through mine, allowing me to pull her to her feet. Her eyes have gotten droopy, and she moves in a slow, silly way, already a little drunk.

"It's *so* cool that you're here," she says, wrapping her arms around my neck. The heat has made her makeup smear. Her face looks like it's melting.

"Thanks," I say, patting her on the back.

"Mara was, like, totally convinced you'd back out. I don't think she really believed you were coming until you stepped off the plane."

The music's louder now, with the sweaty, gyrating crowd pressing in around us. I lean in close to Harper's ear and yell, "Why didn't she think I'd come?"

Harper shrugs, the movement slow and sloppy. "I don't know. I guess she thought your parents wouldn't let you or something? You know what she's like."

Harper suddenly seems distracted by something happening behind me. I turn and spot her art-class friends crowded around the bar. One of the guys peels off his sweaty T-shirt, egged on by some blond girl called Emma or Emily, while the others all press in around him, whooping and catcalling. He tosses the shirt into the crowd, and I have to duck as it flies over my head. Gross.

Harper's eyes have gone glassy. She watches the

sweaty T-shirt sail past and then waves to the blond girl. "Emma! Come dance with me! I *miss* you."

I want to point out that she's spent every single day this summer with Emma, and *I* just got here, but it doesn't seem worth it. Shaking my head, I start to head back to our table.

"*Sei bella,*" someone says. A chill moves from the top of my head and down my spine before settling in the tips of my toes. I turn.

Giovanni's taller than I expected him to be, and his lips curl at the corners, like he's fighting back a smile.

"What did you say to me?" I ask.

His lips twitch. "Ah. An American." The way he rolls his *r*'s makes the hair on my arms stand straight up. He touches a finger to his mouth. His nails are painted in peeling black polish, and he wears a skull ring on his middle finger.

He leans in closer. "*Sei bella* means *you are beautiful.*"

"*Sei bella,*" I repeat. I glance around for Harper—an ugly, jealous part of me wants her to see the dreamy tour guide flirting with me—but she's dancing with the shirtless guy and seems to have forgotten all about me. She stumbles backward, but the crowd catches her, putting her upright again.

Giovanni doesn't ask me to dance, but suddenly his hand is at my waist, and then he's right in front of me.

He smells like something I can't quite put my finger on. Incense, maybe. And smoke.

I want to talk to him, if only so that I can hear that sexy accent one more time, but the music is too loud. The crowd pulses around us, pushing us together. His chest is pressed to my chest, and I feel the heat of him through the thin fabric of my tank top.

He lowers his mouth to my ear and whispers, "I am Giovanni."

"Giovanni," I repeat. His name tastes like chocolate. "I'm Berkley."

"*Berkley.*" In his mouth, my name is a tangle of growling *r*'s and hard consonants. "It is a pleasure."

I don't know what it is, exactly. Maybe the booze has left me feeling dizzy, or maybe it's Giovanni's intoxicating smell, or the foreign music pumping through my veins, making my heart race. Or maybe it's just that I finally feel like someone wants me here. I didn't realize how upset I was until Giovanni curled his arms around me and pulled me toward him.

For a moment, it's like I'm seeing myself from the outside. Sure, my friends sort of ditched me, but I'm still in a tiny bar in Italy, dancing with this gorgeous stranger. I turn my face an inch to the left, and my nose brushes against Giovanni's.

"*Bella,*" he murmurs, moving his face closer to mine.

Just then, the crowd parts. The bartender is watching us from across the room, her brows knitted together, her lips half-curled. I catch her eye. I think I expect her to smile, but instead she shakes her head and goes back to pouring drinks. She looks disgusted.

Giovanni's arm tightens around my waist. The music grows louder. A girl's voice rises above the beat, her scream quickly dissolving into jagged laughter.

I feel a prickle in the air, and for a single second, I find myself wondering what just happened.

But then Giovanni and I are kissing, and I forget the bartender completely.

# CHAPTER 4

Morning comes too early. The smell of lemons and something earthier, like truffles, drifts in through the open window, and I can hear the bustle of people on the street below: horns honking and the sputtering motor of a scooter.

I toss an arm over my face to block the light streaming in from the window and try to will myself back to sleep. My eyelids are lead weights, and it feels like someone's pounding at my head with a hammer.

The door creaks open. "Out of bed, sleepy!"

Mara sounds annoyingly energetic. I groan and bury my face in my pillow. "How are you awake?"

"I got up early to go for a run, and then I read over some of my notes from class last week. I was going to make us some green juice, but Harper said that eating healthy when you're hungover is masochistic, so I guess we're going out." She yanks the curtains open, and sunlight streams into my room, hitting me like a shot. She grabs a T-shirt from my open suitcase, balls it up, and tosses it at me.

"Where did Harper learn the word *masochistic*?" I mutter, pushing aside the T-shirt.

Mara snorts with laughter. "God, you're a bitch. We missed breakfast, but there's a lunch spot down the street that puts eggs on pizza, so it's basically brunch, except with grappa instead of mimosas. We can't wait to hear *all* about your night."

I can't help thinking of Giovanni. My lips still feel swollen from all that kissing. I wiggle my eyebrows at Mara, and she wrinkles her nose.

"Slut," she says, with a slice of a laugh. "Didn't you get enough of him at the trattoria?"

"Define *enough*."

"You'll tell us all about it on the way. Harper's so jealous she wants to die. She still can't believe *you* nabbed the guide."

Her voice lands hard on the *you*. Harper's not the only one who's jealous.

I climb out of bed, grab the T-shirt Mara tossed my

way. Jealousy doesn't bother me. At least now I have a story they want to hear, a reason to keep me around. It helps me feel a little less like the lame high school friend they wish they hadn't invited.

"I'll be out in five," I say.

It's still early, but heat rises up from the cobblestones, filling the air with a haze that makes the sky tremble. Buildings tower over us, blocking the sun, but I manage to catch glimpses of the brilliant blue sky as we twist and turn through the winding streets. I feel like I've stepped back in time. All around me are dark stone buildings and crumbling merchant workshops. The air is thick with the smells of fresh bread and coffee. It makes my stomach grumble.

We walk single file up a narrow sidewalk. Mara and Harper want to hear the story of how Giovanni approached me again and again.

"Did you give him your number?" Mara turns in place, walking backward up the hill.

"He didn't ask for it," I say. Something drips from the sky, landing on my shoulder. I flinch and glance up, spotting balconies crowded with clay pots and overgrown tomato plants and heavy, wet laundry.

"Oh." She sounds disappointed. "Well, that's probably okay."

"I'm sure he didn't mean anything by it," Harper adds.

She doesn't turn around, but she tilts her head toward us, so I know she's listening. I can't make out her expression behind the dark, oversized sunglasses—a completely different pair from the ones she wore yesterday. I have a feeling she bought herself an entire Audrey Hepburn–inspired wardrobe the second she found out she was going to Italy.

"I know," I say. But my cheeks flush. Should I have tried to give Giovanni my number? That hadn't occurred to me.

We stop once we reach the top of the hill. There's a gap in the buildings, and a medieval town spreads out below us like something from a postcard. My breath catches in my throat as I look out over the red brick walls and clay rooftops and an endless labyrinth of cobblestone streets.

Harper pulls out her phone, muttering something about the restaurant being just around the corner. I shield my eyes and look up, catching sight of a low green hill towering over the town. I can just make out the pointy shape of something jutting up from the very top of the hill, silhouetted against the sun.

"That hill is famous," Mara says, squinting. "It was . . . damn, I can't remember the story. What did Professor Coletti say about it, Harpy? Was it Lucia again, or something about the Inquisition? I swear I wrote it down."

"I don't remember, but we can go up after lunch, if you want." Harper frowns at something and then knocks her shoulder into mine, nodding at a man standing on the corner opposite us.

He's young and a little overweight. His belly sags against his blue polo. The red stripe on his trousers and the gun hanging from his belt tell me he's *poliziotto*. An Italian policeman. He watches us, scowling.

"*Puttana americana*," he mutters, shaking his head. He spits on the sidewalk before walking away.

"What's his problem?" I ask.

Harper says, "Some of the locals don't like CART students."

"Especially not us slutty American girls with our short skirts and loose morals." Mara rolls her eyes.

"Just be cool, it's not a big deal." Harper waves her phone at me. "We missed a turn back there. Come on."

Sweat pours down my back as we make our way back down the steep roads and across busy streets that twist and curve, not bothering with stop signs. Cars zip past us, honking like crazy as we approach the street.

"Careful," Mara warns, a hand on my shoulder. "They won't stop for you."

I follow close behind them and jog quickly across the street when there's a break in the traffic. It's harder than I thought it would be to navigate the cobblestones. Harper and Mara don't have as much trouble as I do—they must be used to the bad roads by now—but I struggle to keep up with them, my ankles twisting with each step.

Another slimy drop of water falls from the laundry hanging overhead, slithering down my back. I whirl around, swatting at it like it's a bug, and the edge of my sandal catches a gap in the cobblestones.

I'm falling before I realize I missed a step. I land on my knees—*hard*—the cobblestones rubbing skin from bone. Blood bubbles up from my veins, gathering between my knee and the grimy stones. My ankle pulses where I twisted it.

*Shit.* I grasp my ankle, fighting back tears. Pain pulses below my skin. The strap of my sandal has snapped in half. I look up, expecting my friends to swoop down on me, make sure I'm okay. But they're gone.

"Harper?" I struggle to my feet, careful not to put pressure on my injured ankle. "Mara?"

They were only a few feet ahead of me—they couldn't have gone far. I take a step forward, and pain shoots up my leg. I release a quick hiss of breath, clenching my eyes shut. I need to sit. I'll have to find them at the restaurant, if I can remember what it's called.

A small stone cathedral sits at the end of the twisting road. I shield my eyes to get a better view. Its white-washed walls have long since gone yellow, and a bell tower peeks out from above the other crumbling buildings, casting a shadow over the cobblestones.

Creepy, but pretty. And most churches in tourist cities like this are open to the public, aren't they? I manage to hobble up the stone steps and push the creaky wooden door open.

A thick shadow falls over me. The only light comes from the trickle of sunshine seeping through the stained-glass windows. The space is huge and airless, stretching back much farther than I expected it to. The ceiling soars above, all domes and arches.

A priest in white robes stands at the pulpit at the far end of the room, speaking in solemn Italian to the few people scattered throughout the front rows of wooden pews. I shiver and wrap my arms around my chest.

A girl with acres of dark hair cascading down her back kneels in front of an altar. Above her, hundreds—maybe even thousands—of tea lights flicker, their wicks dancing inside red votive candleholders. I start hobbling toward the closest pew, my ankle throbbing. The girl looks up as I walk past.

She's arresting, but not quite pretty—not like the bartender from last night. A long, thin nose cuts her face in half, hooking slightly over full lips. Her cheekbones are sharp and high, her eyes too large and dark as pools of oil.

*"Scusami,"* she says in a high, tinkling voice, *"sei persa?"*

I hesitate. "I'm so sorry, but I don't speak Italian."

She studies my face, doe eyes narrowing. She wears a modest, ill-fitting dress, the neckline much too high for a day as hot as this one. The fabric bunches around her narrow shoulders and stretches tight across her ample chest. In comparison, my tank top and cutoff shorts show off way too much skin. I feel naked.

She says, in careful English, "Are you . . . sick?"

*Sick.* The word sends something dark twisting through me. I'm not sick. Not anymore.

I say, too quickly, "Why would you think that?"

Her eyes lower, landing on my ankle. The skin around the bone has started to swell and turn purple, and the cuts on my knee are still bleeding freely. Lines of red trail down my leg. Her eyebrows lift.

"Sick?" she says again. Then, searching for the word, "I mean . . . hurt. Are you hurt?"

"Oh! Yes, I'm hurt." I gesture toward my ankle. "Twisted it on the sidewalk."

She shakes her head indulgently and says something else in Italian. She gestures with her hands as she speaks.

"Those sidewalks," she says, in English. "They are the devil. Come here. Sit."

She nods at a chair beside the altar.

*"Grazie,"* I say, sitting.

"Here, light a candle and we can say a prayer, for your health." She points to a sign in front of the candles, written in Italian and English and French. I squint to read the words in the dim light. For a euro, you can buy a candle to light and say a prayer. It reminds me of being a little kid and making a wish as you toss a quarter into a fountain.

"Yes, thank you." I dig a euro coin out of my pocket, but the girl shakes her head.

"No, no. We will give you your first prayer for free." She smiles, her full lips turning up in a demure curve. The smile lights up her face.

I smile back and choose my candle. I think the girl wants me to pray for my ankle to heal, but I can't help thinking of Giovanni's lips, of his hands on my waist. The memory causes heat to rush into my face.

Suddenly I'm making a different prayer—more wish than anything else. It's the same thing I've been wishing for all summer, ever since the moment I got out of the institute.

*I just want to be the person I was before,* I think. *Please let me get my life back.*

The girl stands, lighting a long match, which she hands to me. It trembles as I take it from her, lowering the flame to the candle. I repeat my prayer like a mantra.

*Please let me get my life back. Please.*

The flame jumps from my match to the wick, flaring in a sudden spark of red and orange. I release a surprised yelp and shake the match out before the fire can nip at my fingers.

The girl says something sharp, in Italian, and reaches for my hand. "Sorry," she mutters, pulling my arm straight so she can examine my wrist. "But you should be okay, it is only wax—"

She pauses, frowning. I follow her gaze to a white clump of wax clinging to my arm. She wipes the wax away, revealing pale skin below. The wax didn't leave a mark.

"Strange," she murmurs, brushing the tips of her fingers over my skin. "You are very lucky; the candle did not burn you."

"Yeah." I straighten, goose bumps racing up my arms, and squirm away. "I should go find my friends."

She nods, those dark eyes studying my face with new interest. I back toward the door.

The silence in the church feels heavier than it did a moment ago. I glance up at the pulpit and realize the priest has stopped his sermon. He's staring at me. My breath catches. They're *all* staring at me. The people gathered at the front of the church are twisted around in their pews, watching.

In my hurry to get back outside, I put too much weight

on my ankle and cringe, struggling to push the heavy door open. Heat wafts over me, leaving me momentarily breathless.

I swallow, letting the door slam closed. I hear the Italian girl's voice echo in my head as I struggle down the sidewalk.

*You are sick?*

There's a part of me that wonders if they could tell, if she could smell the institute on me like perfume. If, even now, after all these months, I'm still just the girl in the nuthouse.

I find Harper and Mara sitting outside a little café as I stumble back to the apartment. They make a big show of fussing over my knee, requesting ice from the waiter, and sopping up the blood with napkins.

"We thought you'd gone back home," Harper says offhandedly when I ask why they didn't come to look for me. She's already got a glass of wine in front of her, and I notice that her hangover seems to have disappeared.

I cringe as she presses down on the napkin. Icy water trails down my leg. "Why would you think that?"

Harper and Mara share a look and quickly change the subject.

I tune them out, staring down at the napkin bunched

49

against my knee. The ice has all melted, and my blood has seeped straight through the fabric, staining it red. If I squint, it doesn't look like a napkin at all. It looks like something gory.

Raw meat, maybe. Or a handful of flesh.

# CHAPTER 5

*Before*

I perch on the edge of a white, over-pillowed couch in a small white room. My new therapist has gone overboard with the color scheme. There's white carpet, white chairs, white side tables holding delicate white lamps. Black-and-white photographs cover the walls. Their frames are white. Of course.

Harper did the same thing our senior year, only with black. She painted her walls the color of ink, bought a matte-black bedspread and gauzy black curtains. Hung shiny silver frames on her walls to break up the dark. It looked sort of cool, actually, but then Mara started calling her *goth princess*, so she changed it.

Dr. Andrews takes the seat in front of me and studies me for a moment without speaking.

I study her right back. She's black, in her midforties, with deep brown shoulder-length hair and wide, sympathetic eyes. Everything she's wearing is white. Her eyes are a shade or two lighter than her skin. *Tiger's eyes*, my mother would call them. They're hypnotizing.

"So," she says, folding her hands in her lap. "Why don't you start by telling me why you're here?"

"Here, like, in this office?" I plop back against the pillows. "Daily therapy sessions with you are a requirement during my last three weeks. I figured you knew that."

Dr. Andrews nods. She narrows her eyes just enough to make the corners crinkle. Something about her expression is incredibly calming, like staring into still water. I wonder if they teach that in shrink school.

Mara's thick premed textbooks flash through my head. I bet she'd know.

I clear my throat, waiting for Dr. Andrews to speak, but she only tilts her head, examining me with those strange hypnotist's eyes. The silence grows.

Finally, I ask, "Or did you mean why am I here, like, at the institute?"

She wets her lips. "What do you think I meant?"

I squirm, digging a pillow out from behind my back. "That's all in my file or whatever. Don't they make you study up on us before sessions?"

"They do. But I'd like to hear the story from your perspective." Dr. Andrews leans back in her chair, opening a small notebook. It's a black leather Moleskine, and I don't remember her holding it a second ago, but now it's balanced on her crossed knee, and she has a felt-tip pen in her opposite hand.

I pull one of her pillows onto my lap and start playing with the fringy bit. I expected us to start slowly. Something like "Tell me about your home life" or "Do you have a boyfriend?" I'd almost been looking forward to talking about myself, telling her how my dad used to make us grilled cheese at midnight, our secret ritual. Or how I'd watch ancient Nora Ephron movies with my mom on weekends, the two of us giggling over bowls of popcorn. I'd been normal before all this.

But nope. This lady opens our first session by asking me to give her a breakdown of the worst day of my life. Well, second-worst day.

"It's not a secret or anything," I say, choosing my words carefully. "My friend had just committed suicide. I was sad, and I was at this stupid party, for some reason. I took too many drugs and, like, freaked out or whatever. Had a panic attack. Or 'panic episode.' End of story."

"Is there a reason her death affected you like that?"

"She was my best friend." This comes out more sharply than I intended.

Dr. Andrews lifts her chin. "The mourning process is

different for everyone, of course, but a panic episode seems like an extreme response. Was something else going on?"

I think of Tayla and me at five years old, playing Barbies-meet-dinosaurs in my backyard. The two of us taking a break to run inside for cookies and lemonade. I give a quick jerk of my shoulder. "I don't know. I was just . . . sad. I couldn't stop thinking about it. I feel better now, though, so I don't know why it matters."

I smooth the pillow tassels with my thumb and forefinger, waiting for Dr. Andrews to say something. She watches me for what feels like a full minute.

Finally, she says, "And that's the only reason you think you're here?"

"Well, yeah," I blurt, frowning. "I'd just started college—NYU? I was nearly finished with my first semester when it happened—the episode, I mean. The dean even said I could finish out the year, see how things went, but my mom made me drop out. She wanted me to do six weeks here first, as a precaution. I was hoping that if you talked to me and saw that I wasn't really crazy, you'd see how this was all a big mistake."

Dr. Andrews studies me. I swear, she hasn't blinked once since I sat down. "Is that right?"

"Yeah?" But my voice rises at the end, making it sound like I'm not sure.

Dr. Andrews nods and leans over her notebook.

"What are you writing?" I ask.

She straightens, tapping the edge of her notebook with her pen. "So far, you've told me the reasons other people think you should be here. I want to know why *you* think you should be here."

I feel my jaw tighten. I *don't* think I should be here. I think I should be walking down University Avenue with Harper and Mara, drinking overpriced smoothies and looking through the used books at the Strand.

But, out loud, I say, "Those are the reasons I think I'm here."

Dr. Andrews closes her notebook and places it on her lap, like it's a period she's putting at the end of this particular sentence.

"Therapy is a process," she explains. "There's no way to get through everything we have to work on in one session. Perhaps we'll leave it at that for today."

I dig my fingers into the pillow on my lap.

Sometimes, when I'm in a situation I can't control, I try to think of how my friends might handle it. How Harper would smile and charm her way into getting whatever she wanted. How Mara would use cool logic to point out exactly why the other person was wrong. How Tayla would—

But I don't have those tools. I sit there, silent.

"You can spend the next twenty-four hours thinking

about what you'd like to discuss with me tomorrow." Dr. Andrews places her notebook on the table next to her chair and stands, nodding toward the door.

"Whatever." I get up, tossing the pillow aside, and head back into the waiting room.

The waiting room is a carbon copy of Dr. Andrews's office, except there are half a dozen white chairs scattered around, instead of a couch, and more throw pillows than I've ever seen in one place in my entire life. If I had my phone, I'd snap a pic for Harper. She'd love this.

Sofia sits in one of the chairs, staring into space, knee bouncing like crazy. She looks up when the door opens. "Oh, hey."

"You up next?" I ask.

Eye roll. "Unfortunately."

"Not a fan?"

Sofia goes back to studying some spot on the floor at my feet, eyes unfocused. "Are you?"

"It's only my first session." I glance over my shoulder to make sure Dr. Andrews isn't standing there, listening. The door stays closed, so I drop into the chair next to Sofia and lower my voice. "I was kind of hoping therapy wouldn't be so . . ." I trail off, searching for the right word.

Sofia's eyes come up to meet mine. "Mind-numbingly lame?"

"Something like that."

Her lips purse, like she has a bad taste in her mouth. "Get used to it. The only ways out of here without Andrews's stamp of approval are the three *B*'s."

"The three *B*'s?"

"Bribery, blackmail, or . . ." Sofia sticks her tongue into her cheek, one hand pumping like she's giving a blow job.

"Gross," I say, slapping her. "And whom, exactly, am I supposed to be giving a blow job? If you haven't noticed, there's a severe lack of men in this place."

"Yeah, but it starts with *b*. You're ruining the joke, Berk." She snickers. "What's the big deal, anyway? It's just talking. You told me your story easily enough."

"With her it's *exhausting*. It's like she thinks you should be able to determine your emotional state down to the millisecond."

I catch the twitch of Sofia's mouth from the corner of my eye. She asks, "You sure you told her everything?"

I feel a sudden spike of anger, like a muscle spasm. "You think I lied?"

"Does it matter what I think?"

I force myself to take a beat, lips pressed together tight as I inhale through my nose. I look Sofia full in the face, half expecting to see her laughing at me or at least looking all superior, like she's figured out all my problems in a day of knowing me. But there's not a hint of judgment there. She's got her head tilted to the side, thumb tapping her chin, like she really wants to know what I'll say.

"The deal here is pretty simple," she tells me, after a moment. "Confess your secrets and you're saved."

I squirm in my seat. "What if I don't have any secrets?"

"We *all* have secrets."

It reminds me of something Harper used to say, when the four of us first started hanging out. *Secrets keep you close.* And then she'd wrinkle her nose and wait for us to spill ours, like an offering to the gods of popularity.

Tayla and I gave it, willingly. It never occurred to me that it was weird that Harper and Mara didn't spill their secrets in return.

The office door swings open, making me flinch.

"Berkley," Dr. Andrews says, frowning. "I didn't realize you were still here."

"Just leaving." I stand, catching Sofia's eye on my way to the door. She hops out of her chair and follows Dr. Andrews into her office.

*Confess your secrets*, I think as I step out into the hallway, pulling the door shut behind me. What a weird way to put it. Not *tell* or *reveal*.

*Confess.* Like we're in church.

# CHAPTER 6

## *After*

The three of us are stuffed in the back of a taxi, zipping through narrow streets. One of the CART professors invited a bunch of students over to dinner at his house tonight. Harper got special permission for me to come.

The buildings that fly past our windows look like something out of a fairy tale, all ancient and half-collapsing, somehow more beautiful for their decay. I can't stop staring at them, trying to imagine life behind those cold bricks. Families waking up and making breakfast in those crumbling stone kitchens. Teenagers sneaking in past curfew through those rickety back gates. The sun is setting between the buildings, sending tendrils of bright golden light stretching down the streets. The whole town reminds me of softly smoldering embers.

The taxi doesn't have air conditioning, and the twilight sun beats in through the windshield, leaving the air inside stiflingly hot, even with all the windows cracked and a stale breeze blowing into my face. We take a turn so quickly that I nearly end up on Mara's lap.

I scoot over, lifting the hair off my neck with one hand and fanning myself with the other. My freshly steamed shirt has already started to wrinkle, and the backs of my legs stick to the sweaty vinyl seat beneath me. I brace a hand against the back of the front seat as we fly around another turn.

"You'll get used to it." Harper picks a piece of lint off my shoulder. "Everyone in Italy drives like a maniac."

"I didn't notice," I say, a tiny white lie. Neither of them seems bothered by the drive, and I don't want to be the only one complaining, even if the speed makes my stomach turn over.

Harper raises an eyebrow but doesn't call my bluff. The cab takes a final turn, and then we've left the brick walls of Cambria behind. Green fields filled with cows and wilting sunflowers spread out before us, a tangle of vines in the background telling me there's a vineyard not far away. The road rises and dips with the soft hills.

I breathe a little easier and lean back in my seat. The speed isn't so bad now that we're not twisting through the ancient village streets, tires half on the sidewalk, terrifying pedestrians. The countryside unfolds around us, the heat making the tall grass stiff and brown.

The CART teacher, Professor Coletti, lives in a small house a few miles outside town. His backyard could be from a travel blog, all rolling hills and swaying cypress trees. The sun has just started to dip behind the distant mountains, leaving the evening twilight gold and velvety.

We hear voices as soon as we climb out of the cab, and we follow them to the backyard, where a large group has already gathered.

I don't know what I was expecting. I didn't really get a chance to talk to the other CART students at the trattoria last night, but they reminded me of people I knew from back home. They were dressed in cutoffs and sneakers. They held the delicate, curved grappa glasses like they were shots—and downed them just as easily.

The people gathered in Professor Coletti's backyard seem different. Older, maybe. Or just more sophisticated. The guys all have combed-back hair and ties, and the girls wear dresses, their chignons and buns pinned perfectly despite the heat that makes my own hair frizz. I feel out of place in my wilted shirt. The silk sticks to my back in sweaty patches.

"They're all older, juniors and seniors, mostly," Harper explains, steering me toward a long wooden table beneath an arbor in the middle of the yard. "Mara and I are the only freshmen who knew about the program."

"Thanks to you," Mara says, grinning at me. But her smile seems stretched too tight, and she looks away quickly.

Café lights crisscross the twilight sky, competing with the still-setting sun to illuminate the back garden and climbing grapevines. A group of students has already seated themselves around the table, chairs angled toward an older man, his dark hair shot through with gray, his eyes slightly cloudy behind thick glasses. Professor Coletti, I assume.

"You have to understand, Cambria has spent decades in the most abject poverty. Famine, drought, crop failure, what have you," Professor Coletti is saying, answering a question I didn't hear. He removes his glasses and polishes the lenses with the edge of his shirt. "It's only maybe . . . well, I'd say in the past two or three years that the village has finally started to turn itself around."

"It's history repeating itself," a student I don't recognize adds. "They had similar issues in the sixteenth century, didn't they?"

Professor Coletti points at him, nodding. "Exactly. But back then, they blamed God, didn't they? They told themselves he was punishing them for their sins, and the only way they managed to pull themselves out was with human sacrifice. Luckily, today we have the tourism trade."

A few people laugh. Mara sinks into a wooden chair, sliding her elbows onto her knees as she leans forward to listen.

"What are they talking about?" I ask, nudging Harper with my elbow.

Harper shrugs. "Who knows? Half the stories about this place are all creepy human sacrifice."

Mara tilts her head toward us, eyes still trained on Professor Coletti. "This is that story I was trying to remember earlier. Lucia *was* the one sacrificed on that hill we walked past. It would be fascinating to go up there and see what sort of memorial they have for her."

I think of the hill looming over the town and shiver. *Fascinating* isn't the word I'd use.

Professor Coletti continues, going on to talk about how the CART program floods Cambria with American students—and American *money*—during the summer months. I sway in place as I listen, accidentally shifting weight to my injured foot. Pain shoots up my leg, and I bite down hard on my lower lip to keep from crying out. The swelling has gone down since this morning, but the damn thing still hurts like hell. Nausea floods my stomach.

I suddenly—*desperately*—want to be anywhere but here.

I close my eyes against the pain and nausea, forcing myself to breathe. I tell myself it's just the heat and all the new people. Once I get a glass of wine and sit down, I'll be fine.

I lean toward Harper. "You want a drink?"

She nods, and Mara lifts a finger to show that she'll take one, too.

I head to the refreshment table and take three glasses of wine so white it's practically clear from a girl dressed all in black. It isn't until I shove a few euros into her tip jar that I recognize the tiny tattoos on her hands: stars and moons and a little horseshoe.

"Oh," I say, gathering the glasses up in one hand. The green tips of her hair are easier to make out in the twilight. "Hey."

She's watching Professor Coletti, listening to whatever story on Cambrian history he's telling now. It's a long moment before her eyes flick to me.

She blinks. "Is something wrong?"

"No. I just remember you. You were working at the trattoria last night, right? I'm Berkley."

"Francesca," the girl mutters, but her eyes have a vague look to them, and I get the feeling she's not really paying attention to me. She goes back to watching Professor Coletti.

"These foolish men," she says, almost to herself. "They think they understand us because they know *one* of our stories." She shakes her head and starts furiously polishing a wineglass.

I don't know what to say to that. I find myself muttering, *"Grazie,"* and quickly making my way back to my friends.

Professor Coletti must've finished his story, because the students have shifted into groups of twos and threes, chatting animatedly. Harper and Mara are talking with a dark-haired girl that I vaguely remember from last night, and they don't see me walk up behind them.

". . . from high school," Mara is saying. She has one hand tucked behind her ear, half shielding her face. "She's had sort of a rough summer, so we felt like we *had* to invite her. Is everyone saying it's, like, totally weird that she's here?"

I freeze, my sweaty skin slick against the condensation-covered wineglasses.

The dark-haired girl hesitates. "I think it's more that they don't know why she'd want to come if she's not in CART. Does she even go to college?"

Harper shakes her head. "She was supposed to be at NYU with us, but she took a leave of absence."

"Really?"

Mara leans forward, lowering her voice to a throaty

whisper. "She had a complete mental breakdown. She got sent somewhere to deal with it and everything. But don't tell anyone I told you. She's kind of sensitive about it."

"Shut up, really? Over what? School?"

Harper gives a noncommittal shrug. "Some people can't hack it, I guess."

That's all I need to hear. I veer off toward the garden, my face growing hot. Sweat gathers on my forehead, drawing lines in my makeup as it trickles down my cheeks. The glasses I'm carrying clink together, chilled wine sloshing over the sides.

The conversation I just overheard plays on repeat in my head.

*We had to invite her . . . she had a breakdown . . . she's kind of sensitive . . .*

My heart beats hot and fast. I wait until I'm out of view of the table, and then I abandon two of the glasses of wine on the stone bench and take a deep gulp of the third. The alcohol burns going down, but the aftertaste is sweet and fruity.

I force myself to inhale. The wine helps—some. I take a smaller sip now, my fingers trembling. I'm shaking so badly that most of it has already spilled over the sides of the glass.

Mara made it sound like I *forced* them to invite me.

Like my mommy called their mommies and told them they had to play with me. What a load of shit. If those bitches didn't want me here, they should've said something.

I close my eyes against the anger pounding at my temples. There's no way in hell I'm going back to that table now. Not with Mara and Harper smiling at me and pretending everything's just *fine*.

I picture the two of them looking around for me after a few minutes, growing increasingly agitated when they see that I'm not there, talking in hushed voices about where I might've gone, if they'll get into trouble if I disappear. The thought makes me smile, savagely. Let them worry.

I head into the garden. It's overgrown, with weeds climbing the trellises and wildflowers growing thick around the gate. It looks wild. Unhinged, even.

I don't notice the first statue until I'm standing right in front of it, a crumbling bust of a woman with weeds growing up over her waist. The stone looks old, and the woman's face has almost completely eroded so that only her chin and the vague outline of her brow are still visible. The plaque below the bust reads: *Lucia*.

"Poor girl," I say, taking another drink of wine. I reach out to touch her face when a sudden peal of laughter from the party makes me jump. I jerk my hand away.

Rage curls inside me. What am I doing here? I could be back at the apartment, curled up in my bed with Lucky, icing my ankle, which is still sore from earlier.

I slip my phone out of my pocket and stare at the blank screen. I could get a taxi back to Cambria—I have a few euros crumpled in my pocket—but I don't know the number, and this place seems too far out in the middle of nowhere for cars to just happen by. Do they have Uber out here? I tap my phone screen, thinking I could at least check—

Hands snake around my face, pressing into my mouth. A scream rises in my throat, but the hands press tighter, muffling my voice. Whoever's holding me is *strong*. Every nerve in my body flares, and my heart starts thudding so hard inside my chest that I worry it'll break free.

And then I'm spinning around, and Giovanni is smiling down at me.

I pull out of his arms and smack him on the shoulder—only half-playfully. "You scared me!"

"Ouch." His mouth twists in an adorable grimace, and he pretends to rub the spot where I hit him, eyes devilish in the moonlight. "So sorry I frightened you, bella. I saw you from the road and wanted to say hello."

He nods at the dirt road curving past the edge of the garden. There's a yellow moped propped against the curb.

"What are you doing out here?" I ask.

"Deliveries. I work part-time for the butcher shop." He leans in close, and I smell the cigarettes and wine on his breath as he adds, "I haven't stopped thinking about you since last night."

"Then I guess it's lucky you passed by."

But it doesn't feel lucky. It feels like a sign. Like fate.

Giovanni grins. He hasn't shaved since last night, and the hair shading the lower half of his face looks even thicker. It makes him look deliciously dangerous. "It's not so lucky. This is a small town. Everybody knows everybody. I knew I would see you again."

I close my eyes, letting his words curl like smoke inside me, warming me from the inside out. Everything he says makes me shiver, and every time he's close I feel like my whole body is about to catch fire. Mara and Harper may not want me here. But someone does.

Giovanni's lips part, the tip of his tongue pressing against his teeth. "Want to go for a ride?"

I do. So badly. I glance over my shoulder. The dinner table seems to glow from the middle of the professor's yard, the twinkly café lights surrounding it in a bubble of gold. Mara and Harper sit in the middle of a group of people, laughing.

Briefly, I imagine myself at the table with them. Standing in the circle of light. Giggling at some story. Then the image fades.

They don't want me here. They don't even seem to have noticed that I never came back with their wine, or else they don't care. They're probably relieved to get a few minutes away from their wack-job friend.

*Fuck 'em*, I think, a vicious smile stretching across my face. I refuse to feel upset because Mara and Harper don't actually want me here. I'm in *Italy*. It's time to have some fun.

I tap a finger against the thin stem of my wineglass and then tip the last of the sweet liquid into my mouth. "Let's go."

# CHAPTER 7

Moonlight glints off the moped's yellow paint. It looked bigger a second ago, when I was seeing it from the garden. Up close it's toy-like. A strong wind could knock it over.

I swallow. "You actually ride around on that thing?"

Giovanni comes up behind me and loops an arm around my shoulder. "Is something wrong?"

I love the way he speaks, his voice a rough tangle.

"No," I lie, snuggling in beneath his arm. "I just thought it would be . . . bigger."

Giovanni laughs. It's a deep, sexy rumble that makes all the tiny little hairs on the back of my neck stand straight up. "Bella, are you afraid of my moped?" He kisses my neck, just once, right below my hairline. "You really are an American girl."

"I'm not afraid," I say, which is bullshit. I'm really, *really* afraid. I picture the toy bike peeling out from beneath my legs, the dirt road spinning toward my face, rocks ripping the skin from my cheeks.

And this isn't even a *motorcycle*. It's a motorcycle's baby brother.

But I climb onto the moped behind Giovanni anyway, doing my best to look like I'm absolutely thrilled to ride through the Italian countryside on his little death trap.

*Think of Audrey Hepburn*, I tell myself, picturing Audrey's pixie cut and flapping skirt as she zipped around Rome on the back of a scooter very much like this one. The image makes me a little less nervous as I wrap my arms around Giovanni's waist.

"Where are the helmets?" I ask.

Giovanni twists the grip of the moped, and it makes a sound like a kitten purring. "What for?" he asks.

Oh God. I close my eyes, digging my fingers into the cotton of his T-shirt.

He's laughing as we peel away from the curb.

The moped goes slowly at first, vibrating as it rolls over all the tiny rocks and pebbles on Professor Coletti's drive. Wind whips the hair off my face. I ease my eyes open, just a crack, just to see what's happening . . .

Giovanni twists the moped's grip again, and the tiny bike lurches. A scream rises in my throat, but I bite it back, digging my knees into Giovanni's sides. His T-shirt is a sweaty ball of fabric in my fists.

We go faster. *Faster.* My heart climbs into my chest. I feel . . .

Exhilarated. Like I'm flying.

Giovanni takes a turn, and we whip higher into the mountains. Craggy rocks rise on either side of us, looking nearly black in the darkness. The bike slows as the road angles upward, and then Giovanni twists the handlebar and a deeper roar thrums through the tiny vehicle. We shoot forward, faster, struggling against the incline. The moon hangs straight ahead, a silver orb bobbing in the sky, chasing away the stars. The valleys below are inky black and endless.

I squeal—out of delight, not fear—and curl closer to his body, pressing him between my legs. Vibrations shudder through me, making my bones and teeth clatter. I press my face into the back of his neck, relishing the sweaty, still-warm feel of his skin against my nose and cheek. He tilts his face toward mine, still keeping his eyes on the road ahead, and I feel the rough prick of the stubble on his cheek scrape against my lips.

I can't quite put a finger on the feeling rising inside me. It's not just happiness—it's freedom. I feel freer than I have in forever—since before the institute and everything that happened. I want to throw my head back and shout into the deep, velvety Italian sky.

I whisper in Giovanni's ear, "Let me drive?"

Giovanni doesn't say anything for a long moment. I'm just starting to wonder if he heard my voice over the wind roaring in our ears when he half turns over his shoulder, shouting, "I do not know. This is not as easy as it looks."

"Come on!" I yell back. "When am I going to get another chance to ride a real Italian moped?"

Giovanni shakes his head, but I catch the edge of a smile pulling at his lips, and I know I've talked him into it.

He steers us to the side of the road, where the dry grass has been trampled flat, and cuts the moped's engine. The low buzz seems to hang in the air around us.

Giovanni swivels around in his seat, both bushy eyebrows rising so high they nearly disappear beneath the swoop of his dark hair. "You are sure you want to do this?"

I lean forward, planting a kiss on his nose. "Haven't you heard? Us American girls are all crazy daredevils."

"I have heard that," Giovanni says, winking. He shakes the hair from his forehead and hops off the moped. I scoot forward, the vinyl seat warm where he was sitting.

He slides in behind me, covering my hands with

his hands. His voice is in my ear. "You turn it on like this . . ."

He twists my right hand, and the moped roars beneath me. It sounds a lot louder from the driver's seat. I bite into my lip, grinning like a fool as we roll forward.

"Careful," Giovanni purrs, lips tickling my ear. "We go slow at first, okay? She is delicate."

"Okay." I nod. "Slow."

With Giovanni guiding me, I coax the moped off the side of the road and onto the packed dirt, moving in spurts. It's not nearly as easy as he made it look. Every time I move my leg or twist my wrist, the moped jerks, following commands I didn't realize I'd given.

"You are too tense." Giovanni moves his hands from my hands and rubs my shoulders. "Lighten up, maybe?"

Lighten up. Okay. I can do that. Taking a deep breath, I loosen my tiger-like grip on the handlebars. We roll forward.

"There!" Giovanni squeezes my shoulders. "You are driving like an Italian girl now."

I ease my foot off the brake. We go faster. Giovanni explains how to turn the bike by leaning into it, and the wind blows my hair off my shoulders as we roll around a corner and start heading back down the mountain, the road a steady decline beneath us. Giovanni leans forward and hooks his chin over my shoulder. He moves his hands to my waist, his fingers grazing the inch of space between the bottom of my shirt and the top of my jeans.

"You can go faster now," he murmurs. "It feels like we are moving through mud."

I nod. The fear I'd felt when I'd first slid into the driver's seat vanishes as the road disappears beneath the bike's front tire. I twist the handlebar, and the bike responds with a low growl. We curl around the tiny mountain roads, faster and faster, the wind screaming in our ears. No one is up here but us. It feels like our own private mountain pass. I can't help feeling like the universe made this moment just for me, as a gift after all that time in the institute.

I twist and we go faster. *Faster.*

"Okay, bella," Giovanni says, laughing. "I think we are going fast enough now, yes?"

I nod, but in my head I'm thinking: *Not a chance.* Every time the speedometer climbs a little higher, I feel a twist of triumph in my heart.

I'm fearless. I'm a warrior. I push faster.

"Bella . . ."

The wind steals the rest of his voice. He's just being cautious, anyway, because he knows I haven't ridden one of these things before. He was going *way* faster than this when he was driving. And I've got the hang of it by now. I know my limits.

And I need this. This is everything I've been missing

since the institute. I no longer feel like that zombie girl on all the pills. I no longer feel like I'm not even really alive.

*This.* This is living. This is flying.

The turn up ahead is sharper than the others I've taken so far. I see it coming and inhale, preparing myself. I tilt the handlebars to the side and lean in . . .

But something's wrong. I feel it right away. The balance of the bike is off. I'm tilting too far to the right, and the wheels feel unsteady and slick.

And then—

A horn blares, the noise cutting through all my careful concentration. I look up, and there's a truck rumbling toward us. It's so close. I can't tell where its lane ends and mine begins.

I start to shake, and my tension spreads to the moped, making it tremble between my legs. We're going down. We're going to fall, and the truck is going to run us over. I open my mouth, wanting to scream—

Then Giovanni's hands are curling over mine, and he's pulling the handlebars of the moped back, stopping the skid before it starts. We jolt forward as the bike slows, too quickly, and for a moment a horrible image plays in my head:

*The back wheel skidding out from behind us, sending us into a slide beneath the oncoming truck. Bones breaking . . . skulls crushing . . .*

The truck's horn blares a second time. I clench my eyes shut . . .

And then I hear the truck rumble away, horn still blaring. The danger has passed. I open my eyes again, whipping around to watch the truck vanish up the side of mountain. We didn't crash. We're alive.

"Turn back around!" Giovanni squeezes my hand, which is still wrapped around the bike's handlebars. "Pull over."

I return my focus to the moped. Hands still shaking, I pull the bike over to the side of the road and hit the brake.

# CHAPTER 8

Giovanni insists on driving the moped the rest of the way into the city. I don't argue. My heart still pounds in my ears, drowning out the tinny whirr of the motor. My hands—now grasped tightly to Giovanni's T-shirt—still tremble.

I can't stop replaying what almost happened. The truck's blaring horn. The way the moped tilted beneath my legs, hanging in midair for seconds that seemed to last hours. The ground rushing at my face . . .

I shiver and lean closer to Giovanni. We didn't crash. That's all that matters.

The bike starts to shake as the road beneath us switches

from packed dirt to well-worn cobblestone. Most of the storefronts have already gone dark, but I can still see sausages and cured meats dangling behind the windows, and I can imagine how, in the mornings, the fresh produce must shine with dew beneath the striped awnings. I can taste burnt sugar in the air, but I can't tell where it's coming from until we speed past the darkened windows of a bakery.

Giovanni steers us through the winding streets, slowing to shout *"Buonasera!"* at strolling passersby and pointing things out to me as we ride by.

"There, that is the best espresso in all of Italia." He lifts a hand, pointing to a café that has already closed for the day. A thick padlock hangs from the front door, and wooden folding chairs lean against the walls, but the air still smells of deep, rich coffee. "If you ever want a gelato that tastes like it was made in heaven, you *have* to go there. Promise me?"

The faster he talks, the more pronounced his accent gets. I say, "I promise."

He flicks his hand at me, as though my promise means nothing. "I will take you. Tomorrow, maybe. You will love it."

I can't help smiling as I bury my face into his neck. We speed past a general store with wicker baskets and bunches of fresh basil hanging from the roof. I can see piles of juicy red tomatoes and deep purple eggplant just inside. Giovanni shouts something in Italian to the old woman in the window. She flashes him a wide, toothless smile. And then she looks at me, and her expression darkens.

"*Diavolina*," she mutters, shaking her head. Her left eye is lazy, the dark pupil drifting toward her cheek, but the right eye focuses in on my face.

Giovanni shakes his head, laughing under his breath. "Crazy old woman."

"What did she call me?"

Giovanni slows his moped to a crawl. "It's just a name the old women here call pretty American girls. Means nothing."

We take another tight turn, brick buildings blocking us in on either side. This part of town looks grimier than the rest of Cambria. Clotheslines crisscross the sky above me, stiff, stained towels fluttering in the wind. A sickly looking goat leans against one of the walls. The curved lines of its ribs are clearly defined beneath patchy spots of fur.

At the bottom of the hill, Giovanni cuts the engine and climbs off the moped, offering me his hand. I hesitate. The air down here doesn't smell of sugar and coffee. It smells damp, rotten. Weeds creep up through the cracks in the street. The houses surrounding us look destitute. Half the buildings are boarded up. It's not that late at night, but the windows are all dark.

"Where are we?" I ask, tentatively sliding off the moped.

"This is a famous neighborhood." Giovanni presses one hand into my lower back. "You see that?"

He points at a hill towering over the grimy neighborhood, its shadow casting this part of Cambria in utter darkness. I crane my head back to stare up at it, remembering how Harper and Mara and I walked past the spot earlier today. "That's where Lucia was sacrificed, right?"

"You know our history," Giovanni says, impressed. He snakes both arms around my waist, pulling me into his chest. He's tall enough to rest his chin on top of my head. "Some people say that if you walk there at night, you still hear her screaming."

A breeze blows down the narrow street, chilling the sweat on my arms. I shiver and lean into Giovanni. "Let's talk about something else."

"You don't like our famous story?" He kisses the top of my head. "Most American girls love hearing about Lucia. She lived here, in this neighborhood, you know, a very long time ago."

I wrinkle my nose as I glance around the grimy neighborhood, filled with broken-down buildings. "It isn't very nice, is it?"

Giovanni chuckles under his breath. "No, it is not the

pretty Italia American girls like to see. But come over here. Let me show you something."

Giovanni moves his hand from my waist and heads down a narrow alley. The road is steep, the moon blocked by high walls, leaving the space all in shadow. Water crawls down the bricks, dripping. The sound seems to take longer than it should to reach my ears.

My palms have started to sweat. Giovanni leads me halfway down a dark stairwell. I open my mouth, trying to come up with some excuse to go back home, when he takes me by the shoulders and turns me toward the wall. My words die in my throat.

It's not a wall—it's a *tunnel*, hidden from the street by the angle of the staircase and closed off by a spiky black gate. A brass plaque hangs above it, the Italian words obscured by years of dirt.

"What is this?" I breathe, awed.

"Our catacombs. We buried our dead here after the famine." Giovanni's voice bounces off the walls, then distorts, and continues echoing until it doesn't sound like his voice at all. He reaches through the gate, unlatches something with a click, and pushes it open, hinges creaking. "Would you like to go see?"

The hairs on my arms stand on end. *No*, I think. I most definitely do *not* want to see where Cambria's dead are buried, *thank you very much.*

But I find myself taking a step forward.

The tunnel twists away from the main street, disappearing into perfect darkness. There's a sound like scuffling in the dirt. *Rats.*

I shrink backward. Maybe it's my imagination, but I swear I can see the light reflecting off their tiny red eyes.

Giovanni puts a hand on my back. "This is the spookiest place in all of Italy. You are not curious?"

I swallow. I *am* curious, obviously. The feeling gnaws at me, even as fear creeps over my skin, making my hair stand on end. I take another step into the darkness. And then another.

The tunnel dips lower, and a few crumbling stone stairs appear. I don't hear the scuffling of rats anymore. Maybe we scared them away. Or maybe they're hiding in the corners. Waiting. The thought sends an icy shiver up my spine.

After another few steps, a stone archway curves over us, marking the proper entrance to the catacombs. It's colder here than it should be. Colder than the rest of the city by at least ten degrees. It smells different, too. Rich, like earth and . . . something else. Something pungent that I can't quite put my finger on.

The darkness seems to pulse. I squint, but this darkness is different from what I'm used to. It's the darkness of a place that's never once been touched by sunlight.

I take a step forward, lowering my fingertips to the

walls. They're strange, bumpy, and covered in dust. I move my hands over ridges and crests. There's an open space, like the opening of a very small jar, and then more bumps, something jagged—

I hear a spark behind me, and red light flares up. I cringe at the sudden brightness, blinking. Giovanni has a lighter out, the flame dancing between his fingers. I squint, and the wall comes into focus.

Skulls. Hundreds of them.

They line the walls, stacked one on top of another, starting at the floor and towering all the way to the ceiling, the white bone gone yellow with age. Their dark eyeholes stare out at me, blank and unseeing. Their jagged mouths are broken into permanent grins.

My hand rests on a cheekbone, fingers stretched toward empty eye sockets.

"Oh God!" I jerk my hand away, the skin on the back of my neck crawling. The space seems suddenly airless. I realize that the smell I noticed before, the one I couldn't place, must be human flesh. Long-decayed human flesh.

I must've started shaking, because Giovanni wraps his arms around me. "Bella, bella, no. Do not be frightened." He kisses me on top of my head, rocking me like I'm a child.

"I thought they'd be underground," I choke out, fighting against the nausea rising in my throat. "Like, *buried*."

"It is okay. We can leave now."

I nod and cover my mouth and nose with one hand, but that doesn't make it any better. The smell is still there, pressing against me, creeping up my nostrils. I think I'm going to be sick. I keep my eyes straight ahead as we make our way through the twisting underground tunnels. I try to pretend I can't see the skulls' vacant eyes and broken teeth.

I swear I can hear footsteps down here with us, whispers echoing through the bones.

Giovanni keeps one hand pressed to my back, leading me through the catacombs to another entrance, this one far away from where we came down initially. For a second I wonder how big the catacombs are, but then the darkness opens into a wide square, different from where we entered. We take the small stone stairs two at a time.

Buildings rise around us, grass and wildflowers growing over forgotten staircases, dripping from long-darkened windows. The air here smells blissfully, wonderfully fresh after the catacombs. It's like drinking cool water. The moon hangs directly above, bathing the space in silver.

I turn around and swat Giovanni on the shoulder. "You *rat*. Why would you take me down there?"

He cringes, like I actually hurt him. "I am so sorry. Most American girls love our catacombs."

"Really? Or do *you* love making them scream and go all helpless?"

"Maybe." He shrugs, smiling that devilish smile that curls only one side of his mouth, flashing the tips of perfectly white teeth. For a moment, I forget how creeped out I am. I feel like my knees might crumple beneath me.

"Well. I am *not* most girls."

"Of course not. You are special."

I stop and tilt my head up, looking around. We're in a large piazza. The buildings here aren't all crumbling brick, like they are in the rest of the town. Instead, I'm surrounded by old stone and whitewashed plaster. The structures look mystical bathed in the silver moonlight. I turn in place, awed, drinking everything in. A massive tower stands at one end of the square, jutting into the sky. It looks like a castle. A marble sculpture of a man astride a horse stands at the other end of the square.

But despite the place's beauty, it's empty. The storefronts have been shuttered, and there's no laundry hanging from the windows. The rest of Cambria smells like bread and coffee and sugar, but the air here smells like nothing. It's completely deserted.

Giovanni leads me to a large stone fountain in the middle of the square, long ago run dry. Weeds crawl up around the stone, and rocks and debris fill the basin.

"Where are we?" I stop in front of the fountain and run my fingers over the stone. It's still warm from the day's heat.

"It used to be our main piazza, but the shops all closed many years ago." Giovanni nods to the boarded-up storefronts surrounding the square. "There's been talk of getting the businesses to come back here, now that we have all the students from CART spending their summers here and spending money, but that will take years. It is beautiful, no?"

I nod, feeling a little wistful that I never got to see it in its prime, with shoppers bustling around the square, buying fabulous leather purses and fresh produce from the tiny shops. I think, sadly, of the sterile outdoor shopping center down the street from my house—a Barnes & Noble, a Starbucks, and a J.Crew arranged prettily around concrete fountains and perfectly landscaped greenery. It's a pale imitation of this colorful stone square covered in ivy. "We've tried to build places like this in America, but they never look the same."

Giovanni makes a noise at the back of his throat. "You Americans do not understand architecture. Your buildings are so boring."

I nod, agreeing. "Have you ever been?"

"Ah, no. I do not go to other places." He picks up a rock and tosses it into the fountain. "I am happy here, in Italy. There is good food, good people."

"You don't want to travel?"

"No, not so much. I want to finish school. Get a good job."

I didn't know he was in school. "What are you studying?"

"Business, mostly. A little of this, a little of that." He shrugs with one shoulder. "Cambria is a poor place. It is hard to make money here, except for tourism. That is okay for now, but . . . I want to open a little shop in a piazza like this. Sell things to tourists."

"In Cambria?"

"Maybe. Who knows? The rest of my family has moved to Florence. I think I will go there, too, someday. That way I can help support them."

I want to ask him more about this shop he plans to open, but he puts a hand on my arm, nodding toward the fountain. "Sit with me."

I lower myself to the fountain with him. It might be my imagination, but parts of the stone look darker than others, like they've been stained by something rust-colored.

*Blood*, I think, my mind going back to the catacombs. I shiver and wrap my arms around myself.

"It's weird that there's no one else here," I say, trying to take my mind off those twisting walls of bones. Giovanni gives my hand a squeeze.

"There will be. Tomorrow night is our Festival for the Dead. It is the anniversary of Lucia's sacrifice. People come to us from all over Europe to celebrate and dance. There is music. Wine. Will you come?"

I peek up at him through the fan of my eyelashes, head tilted toward the ground. "Sounds spooky."

"Do not worry, bella. I will protect you." He kisses the skin behind my ear.

"Do the dead crash the party?" I murmur, my eyes fluttering closed.

"No, no. In Cambria the dead are very well behaved."

His mouth travels down my neck and over my collarbone. I moan, leaning closer. Giovanni wraps his arms behind my back and burrows his face in my hair.

"You are so beautiful," he says, and it reminds me of the night we met. Our first kiss. I tilt my head up, and our lips meet.

"*You* are so beautiful," I say, my words getting lost in his mouth. In an instant, I forget why I thought this place was creepy. The darkness, the seclusion . . . it's romantic. Our own private hideaway, accessible only by walking through a tunnel of the dead. Giovanni tightens his arms around me. Kisses me harder until, eventually, I forget the catacombs completely.

I think about the kisses. I can still feel Giovanni's arms twisting around my shoulders, the heat of his chest pressed to mine. I touch a finger to my mouth, trying to remember the warmth of his lips. My eyes flutter close, and my breath catches . . .

A fly buzzes past my ear, the sound of its wings a low

drone. I flinch and jerk away, and my bad ankle twists beneath me, sending pain up my leg.

"Nice one," I mutter to myself, cringing. The last memories of Giovanni's kisses disappear as I hobble the rest of the way home.

It's late when I finally get back to the apartment. I try the doorknob, expecting to find it locked. Harper and Mara couldn't have gotten back from Professor Coletti's yet. But the knob turns easily beneath my hand.

I ease the door open as quietly as possible. I listen for voices but hear nothing. They must've already gone to bed. I take my shoes off and place them next to the door and then creep down the hallway, rolling my feet from heel to ball to keep the floorboards from creaking.

I push my bedroom door open, expecting Lucky to leap off my bed and rub his furry body against my ankles. He's been sleeping on my pillow when I'm not here.

Instead, I'm hit with the smell of something sharp and rotting. I cover my nose with one hand. It takes a second to find the lamp switch, and then a dull, golden glow blinks on.

Someone tore the sheets back from my bed. They ripped my pillows apart, leaving a downy layer of feathers over every inch of my room. A breeze drifts in from the window, stirring them in small drifts.

But that's not the worst part. Whoever did this left me a message.

*Diavolina.*

The word is painted across my sheets in thick, spiky letters, written in something the color of rust, only thicker, and tacky. Flies buzz in through the open window and land on the soiled sheets, wings flicking, crawling over each other. Their eyes look iridescent in the glow of my lamp.

I stare at the sheets for a long time, hand still balled at my nose, eyes watering, until I understand.

The flies. The smell. The tacky, rust-colored paint.

The message was written in blood.

# CHAPTER 9

## *Before*

Mara won't come into my room.

She stands near the metal door, hands clasped in front of her so she doesn't accidentally make contact with the wall. She seems to be trying very hard to keep her nose from wrinkling.

Harper, on the other hand, has taken the opposite approach. Instead of making a face, she keeps her expression perfectly impassive. Like we're hanging out in her bedroom instead of chilling in my dorm inside a fucking mental institution.

". . . and then Cassidy texted his girlfriend exactly what he said, and she broke up with him the next day."

Harper pauses to pick a piece of peeling paint off my wall. They've been here for twenty minutes now, and she's kept up a steady stream of gossip the entire time. "I don't think they're, like, *done* done, but shit got pretty real. I wish you'd been there."

"Yeah." I nod along, even though I lost track of this story at least fifteen minutes ago. I barely knew Cassidy in high school. She was a grade above me, and I never even saw her at NYU, so I have less than zero interest in her love life. "You guys can sit down, you know. They're not going to lock you in here with me."

Mara and Harper glance at each other. Hidden inside that glance is something I'm not supposed to understand, some hint of a conversation they had on the train ride upstate. They take the smallest possible step farther into the room. Seriously, I don't think either of them even really picked their foot up off the floor to move it.

My cheeks burn. I pull my knees toward my chest and loop my arms around them. It's like they think that what I have is catching.

"This place isn't as bad as I thought it would be." Harper dusts off the front of her shirt, even though there isn't a speck of dirt on any part of her clothing. "I was expecting, like, bars on the windows."

"I'm not in *prison*." I try to keep my voice steady, but it trembles a little.

Harper says, her words falsely bright, "Oh, totally. No, I know that."

At the same time, Mara adds, "That's not what she meant."

"Yeah." I stare down at my knees. An uncomfortable silence falls between us. It never used to be like this. We used to FaceTime for hours, interrupting and talking over each other in our desperation to break down every detail of our day. We'd tell the same story three, sometimes four times, always analyzing it from a new angle. Tayla had a hard time keeping up, but I loved those conversations. It was almost competitive, how you had to fight for your chance to talk, and you knew you'd won when the others fell quiet to listen to you speak.

Mom used to cover her ears when Mara and Harper were over, saying she didn't know how we understood each other.

I hear Harper take a deep breath, steeling herself to start up the conversation again. Mara shifts her weight from foot to foot, the soles of her shoes creaking. I bet she's counting the seconds until she can make some excuse to leave.

I can't bring myself to look either of them in the face, so instead I study what they're wearing. Pink T-shirt, white cords, and sparkly boots for Harper. Red minidress with tights and silver Doc Martens for Mara.

I sigh, despite myself. *Color.* I haven't seen this much color since I was admitted.

I self-consciously wrap my arms around my chest. I'm wearing the same colors as the rest of this place. Grayish blue, faded from too many washings. Next to me, Harper and Mara look like flowers.

I look up and catch my reflection in the window as snow falls outside. I can't see myself clearly (we aren't allowed mirrors for some reason that has never made any sense to me), but I see enough to know that my skin has gone dull and that my normally shiny reddish hair hangs around my shoulders in lifeless clumps.

Harper and Mara must look at me and think that I belong here. That I'm one of these girls.

Harper shifts closer to me, breaking up my thoughts. She perches on the edge of my cot, and for a moment, I'm so grateful to her that I could cry.

"So." She offers me a small smile, like a gift. She straightens the bedspread with the palm of her hand. "I've been waiting to tell you . . . I got in."

"You got in," I repeat, slowly. It takes me a long moment to remember what she's talking about, but then I lean forward, my eyes going wide. "To CART?"

Harper nods, her smile widening. "I mean, it's not like they're exclusive, but they *did* say there was an overwhelming number of applicants this year, and I'm only a freshman so it wasn't totally a for-sure thing. They just emailed all my enrollment stuff last week."

"Oh, Harper, that's amazing." I throw my arms around her neck, squeezing, and for a second everything is like it was. I'm not the crazy girl in the mental institution, and she's not my former bestie who acts all weird around me now. We're just two friends, and we could be sitting anywhere. I hold her tighter and say, into her ear, "Cambria's supposed to be a total party town. You're going to have a blast."

Harper exhales, heavily. She's beaming when she finally pulls away. I haven't seen her so happy since she got into NYU. "The town itself is supposed to be adorable. All cobblestone streets and crumbling old buildings. Doesn't that sound gorgeous?"

I nod. "Totally."

Mara inches into the room. She doesn't sit down beside us but leans against my dresser, as though she's still not sure how close she's allowed to get. "Tell her about the apartment, Harpy."

"Oh my God, that's the best part. So, most of the other students are rooming together in this little house downtown. It's super cute, but obviously I couldn't stay there with them, so Daddy helped me find this great apartment right next door. It's inside this old building that used to be a church, and there's all sorts of creepy art and stuff still hanging on the walls. You would die if you saw it, Berk."

I purse my lips, confused. "Why can't you stay in the house with your other classmates?"

"We thought it'd be easier to room together—" Mara stops talking, abruptly, and shifts her gaze down to her shoes. "Shit."

I frown. "What?"

Harper has suddenly become very distracted by a loose thread on her knee. "Mara decided to apply, too."

"You guys made it sound like so much fun," Mara says with a shrug. "I figured why not?"

Harper adds, "It's no big deal."

So that's their big secret. Harper and Mara are spending the summer together, in Italy, attending the art program *I* told them about.

A memory slams into me so suddenly I flinch. Tayla and I are spread across her bed after school, feet dangling over the sides of her mattress, giggling over the grainy pics of Cambria we managed to pull up on her laptop. We order pizza and spend the night arguing over which neighborhood we'd stay in and which coffee shop would become our regular spot, whether we'd date boys from the program or go after locals. For a second, I find it hard to breathe.

Tayla's older sister's best friend did the Cambria

Art Institute summer program a few years back, and she was the one who gave us the heads-up that it was worth the hefty enrollment fee. It's not technically affiliated with any university, so you can sign up to take the course no matter where you go to school. Tayla and I weren't naive enough to think we'd end up at the same college, but we always promised each other we'd meet at CART.

*It's not that big a deal*, I tell myself. Tayla and I told Harper and Mara all about CART after we started hanging with them. We *told them* they should apply; we said the four of us could go together. The plan had seemed so absolutely perfect when we came up with it. The four of us chilling in Italy, drinking wine, meeting boys . . .

But it'd always been *our* dream. Mine and Tayla's. And now Harper and Mara are going together while I'm stuck here. And Tayla . . .

I glance up in time to see Mara and Harper look at each other and then away, clearly not wanting me to see. I shift my eyes back down to my lap, anxiously twisting my fingers together so I don't have to look my friends in the face.

"I didn't even know applications were due," I murmur, almost to myself. I remember looking up the dates with Tayla last year, but I must've lost track of it between the panic episode and coming here.

"We should've reminded you. We just weren't sure what your deal was going to be," Harper explains, after a few minutes of increasingly awkward silence. "With . . . everything."

"CART isn't until the summer," I murmur. It's not even January. Do they really think I'm going to be here for that long?

"Yeah," Harper says. Her cheeks have turned pink. Maybe I should feel bad for her, but honestly, this just pisses me off even more. I'm the one whose entire life is going to shit. What does she have to be upset about?

"Obviously Harper figured you'd be out by then. She meant, like, with school and stuff," Mara cuts in. I look up, sharply. Something about the tone of her voice makes me want to slap her.

She hesitates, frowning at my harsh expression, and then continues, her voice a little softer. "I mean, are you even planning on going back to NYU in the fall? Because you've already missed most of your freshman year. I'm not even sure if you qualify for CART if you aren't currently enrolled in classes. And do you really think your parents would let you travel abroad? After—"

"I was committed?" I snap. Mara swallows and shifts her eyes back to the floor.

The door to the dorm room opens, and all three of us flinch. But it's just Sofia.

"Oh, look. Outsiders," she says, mouth twisting in a way that could've been a grin if she weren't showing so many teeth. She looks at me. "You going to introduce us?"

"Harper, Mara, this is my roommate, Sofia. Sofia, I know Harper and Mara from high school." I pause for a second, then add, "We've all been friends forever."

"Hey," Harper and Mara mumble in unison. Harper coughs and pretends to be distracted by a spot on her cords. Mara can't stop staring at the serpent tattoo in the crook of Sofia's hand.

Can't really blame her. The tattoo looks particularly disturbing right now, with the harsh overhead lights flickering down on it, making it look like the blue lines are moving. Sofia's skin has gone all red and puffy—I think it might be infected.

"It's so nice of you to come visit Berkley in here," Sofia says, voice falsely bright. Her eyes bounce from Harper to Mara, one eyebrow going up when neither of them looks back at her. "You must be *really* close."

She starts picking at the scab forming around her tattoo. I think she's just doing it to freak them out.

Mara stares, a muscle at the corner of her eye twitching. "Yeah," she says, distracted. "The best."

I try again. "Sofia's from Mississippi. Harper, didn't your mom grow up there?"

"Yeah, but we never go back." Harper's nose wrinkles,

just a little, before she seems to realize what she's doing and wipes the expression from her face.

The silence stretches a beat too long. I should say something else, try make this easier for everyone. But I can feel my heartbeat pounding in my ears, blocking out the rest of my thoughts.

"I think . . . probably we should be going," Mara says, giving Harper a very intentional look. Harper pushes herself off my bed.

"Yeah, we have this lunch thing . . . Anyway, we'll visit again soon, Berk." She follows Mara out the door, and the two of them dart down the hallway so quickly you'd think someone was chasing them.

I dig my stubby fingernails into the mattress as I watch them go, feeling more lonely and lost than I have since I first got to this hellhole. I picture them finding the nearest subway on their phones, taking a train into Manhattan, just like the four of us used to on weekends back in high school when NYU was just a dream. It's not even forty minutes away from here.

They'll meet one of our old high school friends for lunch, grabbing a gooey slice of pizza from Artichoke or braving the epic Shake Shack line for burgers and fries, like old times. They'll giggle and gossip—probably about me.

The thought fills me with jealousy, but at the same

time, I wish they'd told me who they were meeting. I wish they'd told me where they were eating and what they planned to order. As I much as I hate them for moving on without me, I want to soak up every detail.

I sigh and say to Sofia, "You couldn't have waited to pick at your gross tattoo scabs until they were gone?"

"Why?" A small smile twists her lips, like she knows something I don't. "You worried they'll think I'm *crazy?*"

Her eyes go cartoon-character wide on the word *crazy*. I lower my head to my hands, digging my fingers into my scalp. "*God.* Never mind."

"Don't be so dramatic. What's CART?"

I stare at her through the cracks in my fingers. "You were *listening?*"

"You weren't exactly being quiet. Is it like a study-abroad thing?"

"Art program," I mutter, not looking at her. "In Italy. I was supposed to go, but . . ."

I shrug. I don't want to talk about this now, not with her.

Sofia leaves the silence for a beat, then groans. "I don't know why you're getting all pissy. They already thought I was crazy, Berkley. They thought I was crazy before they ever met me."

"You don't even know them."

"Girls like that are all alike. You think they're your

friends now, but . . ." Sofia trails off, staring at the wall behind my head. "They'll never look at you the same after this. You know that, right?"

A shiver moves through me. I try to ignore it, but the cold wraps around my spine and squeezes.

*They'll never look at you the same.* I suddenly want to scream. I want to throw things. How is it that she was able to pinpoint the exact thing I've been obsessing over? Am I so obvious?

"You're wrong," I say, plopping back on my mattress. The pillow flattens beneath my head. "They're my best friends. They know I don't belong here."

I force myself to stare at the pipe running across the ceiling instead of looking over to see her reaction. Water drips down in a single perfect droplet. It smells putrid, like sewer, but I don't bother wrinkling my nose. I'm used to it by now.

After a moment, Sofia says, in a small voice, "If you say so."

# CHAPTER 10

## *After*

I don't know how long I've been screaming. My throat's gone raw, and my ears ring with the sound of my own voice. I can't look away from my bed, can't tear my eyes off that word.

*Diavolina.*

Another fly buzzes in from the open window. It seems to move in slow motion, hovering in midair, wings trembling as it lands in the pool of blood gathered between the folds of my sheets.

I dig my fingernails into my cheeks. It feels like my hands are the only things keeping me from falling apart. My stomach clenches, and an acid taste rises in my throat.

I'm vaguely aware of thumping footsteps and voices vibrating down the hall. My door slams open. Hands grab my shoulders, shaking me.

Harper shouts, "Berkley? Berkley, *please* stop screaming. What's going on? What happened?"

And then Mara: "Oh my God . . . Harper, did you see? Oh my *God*."

I clench my eyes shut, press my lips together, and force myself to breathe in through my nose. I feel dizzy. My knees shake like crazy, struggling to hold me up. My own screams still echo in my head.

When I open my eyes again, Mara and Harper are staring at me.

"It was like this . . . I just got . . ." The taste of vomit clings to the back of my mouth, and the metallic smell of blood clogs my nose. I swallow. Try again. "I don't know . . . who would have . . ."

"It's okay." Harper's voice is half-freaked, half–nursery school teacher sweet. She drops a hand on my shoulder. "Let's sit, okay? Can you sit?"

Mara doesn't look at me, but the lines of her shoulders have gone rigid. She leans over my bed, plugging her nose with one hand as she rips away the soiled sheets and tosses them into a pile. "Nasty," she mutters under her breath.

I sink to the floor, pulling my knees to my chest. Harper crouches over me.

"How about you start from the beginning?" She squeezes my shoulder and starts rubbing in slow circles. "What happened?"

Another deep inhale. "I . . . I just got home. The window was open." I nod at the open window. "I didn't think it was weird because I've been leaving it open so Lucky can get in, only Lucky wasn't here this time. The light was off, but I noticed the smell when . . ."

Harper frowns. "What does the window being open have to do with anything?"

"That must've been how they got in!"

Mara and Harper share a look. Harper says, slowly, like she's speaking to a child, "You think someone climbed into your window and did this?"

"Well, yeah," I sputter. How else could it have happened?

Mara raises an eyebrow, head tilted like she knows something I don't. She's blinking very quickly. "Why would someone do that, Berkley? You don't even know anyone here."

I stare at her face for a long moment before realizing . . .

She thinks *I* did this. She thinks I'm so sick I would paint my bedsheets with blood.

I curl my fingernails into my palms, taking comfort in the flare of pain that shoots through my skin. "What exactly are you saying?"

This time, they make a point of *not* looking at each

other. Mara frowns down at the floor. Harper picks at something beneath her fingernail.

"I'm not saying anything." Mara flicks an icy blond strand of hair behind one ear. She's still using a voice that suggests she's smarter than I am. Like I couldn't possibly understand her. "But you have to admit, it's kind of—"

Harper shoots Mara a look, and she stops talking, abruptly.

"It's kind of what?" I say. Neither of them answers, so I ask again, louder. "I have to admit, it's kind of *what?*"

Harper says, her voice low and tired, "What are we supposed to think, Berkley? You've been weird all day. You got lost on the way to brunch, and when you finally do show up, you're completely covered in blood. Then you ditched dinner without telling either of us."

"You have no idea how worried we were," Mara says. "We had everyone looking for you. We almost called the police."

My eyes shift to Mara, and I open my mouth to explain. She's staring right at me now, eyes narrowed in distrust. It's like she doesn't recognize me.

I feel my spine tense. "You both have clearly already made up your mind about me." I push myself to my feet—too fast—and head for the door. Something throbs in the palm of my hand; it feels like my heartbeat.

Maybe there's a hostel still open somewhere. Or else

I can sleep on a park bench. Anywhere is better than here.

"You were with that guy again," Harper blurts as I wrap a hand around my doorknob. "The tour guide guy."

"Giovanni," Mara adds.

"So what if I was?" I exhale and turn around. "Is it so wrong to want to spend what's left of my summer hanging out with someone who actually wants me around?"

"We want you around," Mara says, exasperated. "Why else would we invite you here?"

My anger flares. *Liar.* "Give it up, Mara. I heard you talking about me back at that dinner." I let my voice go higher, mimicking. "Berkley had a *breakdown.* We had to invite her. We don't even know why she came."

Mara's skin goes a shade paler. "That's not what I said—"

"It's *exactly* what you said!"

"Stop it, both of you!" Harper cuts in. She lets her hands fall open beside her, shoulders sagging. To me, she says, "You shouldn't have heard that. It was really shitty of us to say those things. I'm so sorry, Berkley."

I open my mouth. Close it again. Not what I was expecting.

"We *were* really worried about you," Mara adds in a softer voice. "You just disappeared in the middle of dinner, and nobody knew where you'd gone. We left Professor

Coletti's early to come look for you. We only figured out you were with Giovanni because of Francesca, that bartender chick at the party, remember? Anyway, she saw the two of you riding around on his moped."

She looks genuinely concerned. I feel my anger start to fade.

Maybe I'm being too hard on them. It's not like we've had some big heart-to-heart since I got out of the institute. They don't get how it feels to suddenly be free after being locked away like an animal. How I want to live all at once, right now.

I groan and rub the space between my eyes with my thumb. Our fight seems stupid now. I'm overreacting.

"I'm sorry I ditched you," I mumble after a moment. "I freaked out after I heard you guys talking."

"That's fair," Harper says. "I can't even imagine how that must have felt."

Mara rubs her eyes with two fingers. "Look, we're all stressed and seriously freaked out by this." She motions to the pile of sheets on the floor. "Let's get some sleep and try again tomorrow. We still have time to do Italy right."

"And tomorrow is the Festival for the Dead," Harper adds. She crosses my room and opens the wardrobe door, pulling out a stack of fresh white sheets. "People come from all over Italy to attend. It's sort of famous."

"It's *crazy* famous," Mara adds. She turns to me, tentatively. "Want to go with us?"

Harper cocks an eyebrow.

There's still a part of me that wants to tell them no. Watch their faces fall as they realize *I'm* rejecting *them* for once. But then I think of how hard it will be to find a hostel now. How I really don't want to sleep on a park bench. I look around my room, realizing I've come to like the small coziness of it. I don't want to leave. And they *are* trying. It might not be perfect, but it's something.

"What kind of person comes to Italy without hitting up the party of the season?" I say after a moment.

Mara bites back a smile. "It's a date then."

"Sure. It's a date."

I start to help Harper tuck the fresh sheets around my mattress. Mara joins us a moment later, gathering downy feathers in her hands and pulling pillows out of soiled cases. Together, the three of us remake the bed, removing all traces of blood and flies and feathers. Harper takes the ruined sheets with her when she goes. I don't think to ask her what she's going to do with them.

I thank them and say good night. After they leave, I change into my pajamas, brush my hair, and wash the sweat from my face. I try not to look directly at the bed, but I keep catching glimpses of those clean white sheets in the mirror or from the corner of my eye. They're always there, flickering at the edges of my vision, and I have to whip around fast to make sure that word isn't still written across them.

*Diavolina.*

I don't know any Italian, but even I can figure out that it means *Devil*.

# CHAPTER 11

Mara holds up a red dress covered in sequins. It's got long, bell-shaped sleeves, and the sequins are oversize, garish.

Harper makes a noise like she's choking. "*Please* put that hideous thing back where it came from."

"It's not that bad," Mara says, frowning.

"Are you kidding?" Harper shoots back. "I can barely keep my breakfast down. Have I taught you *nothing*?"

Mara thrusts the dress back on the rack, rolling her eyes. "So what's the deal? We can either be a slutty devil or slutty angel?"

"I think the options are *devil* or *angel*, but yeah, that's the general idea." Harper considers a lacy white slip dress, wrinkles her nose, and then places it back on the rack. "Too bad everything here is so *boring*. I thought Italy was supposed to be all about fashion?"

I tilt my head, studying the dress Harper just discarded. I sort of see what she means. I bet all the girls at the party will be wearing some skimpy, silky thing, glittery wings drooping from their backs.

I didn't realize the Festival for the Dead was a costume party until Harper shook me awake this morning and told me it was time to go shopping. Apparently there's even a contest later in the evening, with prizes going to the group with the most interesting interpretation of angels and devils. Mara told us that last year's winners were a bunch of Swedish girls who showed up in their underwear, claiming to be the Victoria's Secret Angels.

"What if we did Charlie's Angels?" I ask, holding up a pair of tight shorts. There isn't a costume shop in Cambria, so we're at some cheap clothing place with a name I can't pronounce. It feels like the Italian equivalent of Forever 21. "We'd have to find roller skates."

"Who're they?" Mara mutters without looking up from the rack she's flicking through. She's made her way over to the lingerie section—probably thinking of the Victoria's Secret Angels, too. I sigh and put the shorts back.

"Or we could be daredevils? We could wear leather jackets and aviator sunglasses? That might be kind of cool."

Harper frowns. "You want to wear *leather*? In this heat?"

She has a point. I join Mara next to the lingerie and pick out a lacy black teddy. "What if we wore the jackets over nothing but this?"

I'm half joking. But Mara freezes, raising both eyebrows at once. Harper purses her lips.

"That could be cute," she says, taking the teddy from me.

"We could add little devil's horns," Mara says.

"And studded heels. We could be, like, biker devil babes."

The idea of waltzing into a party wearing nothing but underwear and a leather jacket horrifies me.

Harper looks over, as if sensing my reluctance. "What do you think, Berk? You'd look hot in the black."

She tosses the black teddy to me and smiles with her lips pressed together, eyes flashing. It feels exactly like being dared by a naughty child.

It *was* my idea. I'd look like a total spaz if I backed out now.

"And sunglasses," I add, grabbing two more teddies. "*Aviators.* Otherwise no one will get our costume."

"Genius," Harper says, nudging me with her shoulder.

I feel a quick dart of warmth as I make my way over to the accessories section.

The streets are packed by the time we finish. Students and families press around us on all sides, making their way to the piazza to find a spot. Stands have already sprung up on the sidewalks, selling fresh fruit and vegetables, sharp, hard cheeses, and thinly sliced meats sandwiched between crunchy rolls of bread. Somewhere in the square, there's a pig roasting on a spit. The salty smell of meat hangs in the air, making my stomach rumble.

The festival lasts all day. There's a parade before the party, and musicians have already piled onto the sidewalks, strumming guitars and singing in deep, throaty Italian. A man with a little girl on his shoulders walks past us. She has angel's wings strapped to her back, and the glitter catches the sunlight, making her seem to glow.

"This is literal hell," Mara moans, pushing the sweaty hair back from her forehead. "At this rate we won't get home until *dinner*."

"Let's go this way." Harper grabs me by the elbow and steers me down another walkway, this one twisting away from the piazza and blessedly free of people.

Mara asks, "Doesn't this lead away from the apartment?"

"Yeah, but it connects with Via Acquasanta."

"Not for, like, a mile. Isn't Via Norcia closer?"

They pull a little ways ahead, muttering about *Via this* or *Via that* as we make our way through the streets. Every now and then we pass a small group of chattering people headed back the way we came. I don't bother trying to help. In the two days I've been here, I haven't once tried to navigate the town without Harper and Mara or Giovanni to guide me. I don't know how they find their way around. The city feels like a maze to me, with streets tangling and twisting around each other, the buildings all towering over me, looking identical. Half the time, I expect to turn a corner and find that I've stumbled upon a secret entrance to Narnia or Westeros.

After a while, even I can tell that we're lost.

"Maybe we should ask for directions?" I ask, stopping in front of a butcher shop. A giant dead pig dangles in the front window. Its face is pink and masklike.

Giovanni mentioned doing deliveries for a butcher shop. I look around, but I don't spot his yellow moped among the dozen or so parked out front.

Harper considers the dead pig in the window, her lip curling. For a second I think she's going to argue. But then her shoulders sag, defeated. "Yeah, okay."

The pig turns slowly in place, its black eyes watching us approach. I suppress a shudder. Holding my breath, I push the door open.

A girl about my age looks up. She's Italian, obviously, and much larger than any girl I've ever known. She must be over six feet tall, with broad shoulders and arms muscled like an athlete. Dark hair falls just short of her shoulders in thick, bushy tangles.

"Ciao, can I help you?" she asks, not smiling. Her nose is a hair too long, but not in a way that makes her look homely. In fact, it gives the rest of her face an arresting quality. She looks like an Amazonian warrior.

"Ciao, ciao." Harper leans across the peeling linoleum counter and shows her the map on her phone. Some of the irritation fades from the girl's face as Harper explains our dilemma in flawless Italian.

I turn in place while they talk, casually searching for signs of Giovanni. My sneakers crunch against the thick layer of sawdust covering the floor. The shop smells heavily of blood.

The girl seems to be alone here, surrounded by dead animals, horseflies buzzing around the meat. I wrinkle my nose. I don't know how she can stand it. The meat hanging from the ceiling is mostly torsos and legs, which isn't so bad, but the display case holds row after row of animal skulls, pink flesh still clinging to the bones.

I hover a few feet away from the case, lip curling. No one bothered to remove the eyes from the skulls. Something that looks like it used to be a goat stares up at me. Without lips, its teeth are bared in a permanent snarl.

A hand touches my elbow.

I flinch and whirl around. "Jesus," I breathe when I see that it's just Mara. "You scared the shit out of me."

"Yeah, this place is disgusting." She glances at the display case and shivers. "Let's go."

She and Harper hurry out of the shop, but I lag behind. The butcher shop girl drums her fingers against the counter, watching me with flat, empty eyes. I shiver, thinking that her eyes remind me of the dead goat's.

"Did you want something else?" the girl asks after a moment. Her voice is deep and throaty.

"Yeah, hi. Uhm, I'm Berkley?"

The girl blinks. After a moment, she says, "Elyse," through clenched teeth. Her apron is stained with dark reddish-brown spots.

*Blood.* My stomach turns. "I'm sorry, I'm friends with Giovanni. I just thought that maybe he works here?"

Elyse considers me, saying nothing. Then she steps away from the counter and removes a butcher's knife from the metal strip attached to the wall. Its sharp blade gleams in the fluorescent light.

"So what if he does?" She shrugs in a slow, lazy way and pulls a small animal carcass from a hook dangling off the ceiling. The animal looks fresh, its meat still bright pink.

She slaps it onto the butcher-block counter, picks up the knife, and slams it into pink flesh. Gleefully.

I flinch, letting an awkward moment pass as Elyse butchers the animal, her movements practiced and precise. She separates meat from bone with quick flicks of her blade. She wipes blood on her apron like it's nothing.

Finally, I clear my throat. "Is he here now?"

"Who would like to know?" she asks, eyes flicking up to me.

I swallow, but I can't look away from the half-butchered creature. Without skin, it's hard to tell what kind of animal it was. Too small to be a pig. A rabbit, maybe.

Or a cat.

My stomach clenches. Lucky never returned to my room last night. And all that blood had to have come from somewhere.

Nausea rises up in my chest, filling my throat. I'm going to be sick. I shake my head, muttering "Never mind" before hurrying back to the entrance. I push the door open—

"*Diavolina.*"

Nerves crawl over my skin. I look over my shoulder. "Did you say something?"

Elyse raises a heavy black eyebrow. There's a spray of blood across her cheek. It looks almost pretty against her dark skin and black eyes.

She shakes her head. "No. I didn't say anything."

# CHAPTER 12

## *Before*

There's something dark crusted beneath my finger-nails.

I pick at it with my thumbnail, pressing so hard that the jagged edge cuts into skin, making it sting. It looks like dirt. Or blood, maybe. It could be anything, in this place.

"You're going to be sitting here for the remainder of the hour anyway." Dr. Andrews taps her pen against the edge of her notebook. "You may as well talk to me."

I drop my hands onto my lap. Everything around me is white and curated and perfect. It makes me even more aware of my own grubbiness. The scrubs that haven't been washed in a week and my hair, all dry and frizzy from the cheap shampoo they keep in the showers. I can't remember the last time I saw my reflection, but I feel a zit pressing through the skin just above my eyebrow, the bump raw and painful to touch.

Back home, I have an entire closet of beauty supplies. Shampoos that smell like coconut and Korean sheet masks decorated to look like animal faces and tiny bottles of tea tree oil ointments that make my zits disappear overnight.

I curl one fist around the other. I can't see the dirt beneath my fingernail anymore, but I can feel it. It pulses at the tip of my finger, like a second heart.

I swallow and force my attention back to Dr. Andrews's face. "I'm sorry, what did you say?"

Dr. Andrews lifts both eyebrows in tandem. "I asked you why you're here."

I roll my lower lip between my teeth. I should just ignore her. The thought of silently counting down the minutes until she has to let me sulk back to my room fills me with a kind of terrible glee. Tayla and I did that once, after we got caught ditching PE, the one and only time either of us ever skipped a class. The vice principal called us into his office, demanded to know where we were. We claimed period cramps and then gave him stone-faced silence for the next twenty minutes as he told us that he didn't believe us, that he was going to call our parents, that we were getting suspended. Eventually, frustrated with our refusal to defend ourselves, he just let us go. The two of us giggled about it the entire way home.

It's not like these sessions have done anything for me anyway. I'm only here because I have to be.

I plop back against the fluffy white pillows. "Why am I here?" I repeat. "You ask that question every time."

"And you still haven't answered it."

I shift my gaze to the clock on the wall above Dr. Andrews's head. The short hand points to the one, and the long hand has just twitched a hair closer to the eight. 1:39. Only twenty-one minutes left in this session.

I blow a frizzy lock of hair off my face. It's my sixth—and *final*—week at Mountainside. Which makes this my second-to-last session with Dr. Andrews. May as well go out with a bang.

I say, "I told you about my friend Tayla. The one who . . ."

Dr. Andrews leans forward, elbows sliding to her knees. "You've mentioned her."

"We were friends." The words come easily, like they've been waiting for their chance to escape. "In grade school and middle school, we were best friends. Practically inseparable. And then we got to high school and things got . . . I don't know . . . complicated."

"Complicated?"

I think of Mara and Harper and me at the lunch table, giggling under our breath at the oh my God *so* dumb thing Erik Masters said in homeroom, gossiping about how Todd Harrison was *totally* cheating on Marissa Clark and how could she not know?

Tayla listened with a sour expression on her face, judging us. Afterward she pulled me aside, told me I'd changed.

Her voice was desperate and confused. *"When did you get so mean?"*

I don't realize I've started picking at my finger again until a sharp jab of pain pricks the skin beneath my nail. I wince and slide both hands under my thighs, digging my fingers into the fabric of the couch.

"Berkley?" Dr. Andrews urges.

I say, in a rush, "You know how some people are, like, weirdly perfect? Tayla was like that. She got straight As in school, made the varsity volleyball team her sophomore year. She got into Columbia. She would've gone in the fall, if she hadn't . . ." I pause to take a breath. "If she hadn't committed suicide."

The word hangs in the air between us for a long time. I look up and see Dr. Andrews watching me. She doesn't look surprised, just patient, like she's waiting for me to say something deep and profound.

"Were you jealous of her achievements?" she asks.

I feel my lip curl. "No. You don't get it."

"Then help me understand."

I think of Tayla skipping Harper's birthday party junior year because it was the night before a big chem test and she wanted to study. Tayla going out for yearbook even though Mara teased her about it endlessly. "I just want you to know what kind of girl she was."

"And what kind of girl were you?"

*I wasn't stupid enough to miss one of Harper's parties,* I think. I slide a hand out from under my legs, grasping, like I might pluck the right words straight out of the air. "I was . . . I don't know. Different."

"You didn't care about school?"

"I did, it's just . . ." I close my eyes, frustrated. She isn't getting it. "Tayla cared way more than she was supposed to. This one time, she got a 98 on a test instead of a perfect 100. After class, she ran into the bathroom and cried. Over *two points*."

"And you think that's why she killed herself?"

I shrug with one shoulder. "Not over that exact test, no. But yeah, I figured the stress of school had something to do with it. She didn't leave a note or anything, so no one really knows why she did it."

Dr. Andrews writes something down. Underlines it. "How did her death affect you?" she asks without looking up from her notebook.

I remember my mom knocking on my bedroom door, red-eyed, her voice raspy and strange. *Honey, I have something to tell you. It's about Tayla.* The way the world seemed to stop spinning after that moment. How time stood still.

I press my lips together. "It didn't."

Dr. Andrews lifts her eyes without raising her head.

"I mean, I guess it freaked me out a little. It always seemed like Tayla had everything under control, and then it turned out that she couldn't deal. It made me wonder if . . ."

I don't finish the sentence. Dr. Andrews leaves it hanging for a beat and then says, "If . . . ?"

"If I was going to end up like her, I guess." My voice sounds very small. "If I was going to crack, too."

Once, the four of us were hanging out in the gym after school. The gym's in the old part of the high school, and it hasn't been updated in something like fifty years. Bleachers wrap around the edges of the room. They're old, made of wood instead of aluminum, and when the basketball hoop is lowered, you can see the other side of the backboard. For years, kids have written things there, signed their names, or drawn pictures.

We all wrote on the backboard that day, using these bright pink and green Sharpies Mara stole from the art room. Harper and Mara left thinly veiled pieces of gossip. I just wrote my name: *Berkley was here!*

But Tayla . . . she wrote these old lyrics from some song I didn't recognize. *I've been afraid of changing because I've built my life around you.* We made fun of her, but she didn't care. She signed her name beneath it, proud.

She was so sure of who she was, who she wanted to be. It never occurred to me that she could break.

Her mom played that song at Tayla's funeral. She said it used to be one of their favorites.

I close my eyes, and it's not until my eyelashes press into the tops of my cheeks that I realize they're wet. I'm crying. I brush the tears away with a jerk of my hand.

I hear the sound of a notebook slapping shut. The click of a pen. Then, "I'm really proud of you, Berkley. I think this is a breakthrough."

I open my eyes again. "Does that mean I'm getting better?"

"I think it means that you've done some good work today and that you should be proud of yourself." Dr. Andrews smiles. "Next session, let's start talking about some strategies you can incorporate into your day-to-day life when you get back home. Ways not to let the pressure get to you, so to speak."

The soft curl of her lips sends a shock of hope through my chest. *Back home.* I've barely let myself imagine it. It's like I thought I might jinx myself.

But now . . .

Now it feels real.

• • •

Sofia sits in the waiting room, slouched on the off-white chair. She has a cream-colored pillow on her lap, and she's idly flicking the tassel with her thumb and forefinger.

She curls her hand around the tassel as I walk past, and her eyes shift to my face. "You look happy."

"My six weeks are almost up." I replay Dr. Andrews's words—*back home*—and a shiver of anticipation moves down my spine. "I guess I'm just excited to get out of here."

Sofia stares at me, not blinking. Her eyes have that empty look they sometimes get, like there's nothing behind those inky black pupils but space. She asks, "What makes you think you're getting out?"

"Just some stuff Dr. Andrews said." I shrug, looking at the wall behind Sofia's head. "She thinks I'm making progress."

"So you finally told her the truth?"

My lips twitch. "A . . . version of it."

"What's that mean? A *version*?"

"I told her everything she needs to know."

Sofia releases the pillow tassel. For a moment she's silent, watching it spin as the tangled threads unwind. I'm halfway to the door when she reaches out, fingers wrapping around my wrist. "You're not going home. You know that, right?"

I shake her off with a jerk. "How is that your business?"

"Rule number one of this place: no lying. They catch you in a lie and you're totally fucked." She holds both hands up, all innocence. "I just thought you should know."

"I *didn't* lie."

Sofia laughs, a single dry scrape. "But you didn't tell the truth either. Not the whole truth."

I feel my chin jut out, same as it used to when I was ten years old and Dad caught me in a lie. The thought causes a hot rush of blood to shoot up my neck. "I told her what happened. What difference does it make if I left out some of the details?"

"Trust me. I've been here long enough to know what they're going to freak out about. You have to tell them *everything*. They'll know if you don't." Sofia shrugs, hands dropping back into her lap. "I'm not making this shit up."

I think of what she said to me the first time we met. *They're never letting me out.* "If you're such an expert, then why are you still here? Why not confess your secrets or whatever and go home?"

Sofia still doesn't blink. "I *am* going home."

*Bullshit*, I think, but the door to Dr. Andrews's office swings open before I can say the word out loud.

"Sofia, how nice to see you again." Dr. Andrews holds her white cardigan closed with one hand and beckons Sofia with the other. "Why don't you join me?"

It isn't until Sofia has disappeared into Dr. Andrews's office, the door closing firmly behind them both, that I realize I haven't moved a muscle.

*There's only one way out of here . . .*

*Bullshit*, I think again. I pull the door open, shaking the nerves from my arms.

But Sofia's words echo through my head as I wind through the institute's cold hallways, making my way back to our room.

*They catch you in a lie and you're totally fucked.*

# CHAPTER 13

## *After*

The crowd of people in the streets has multiplied by the time we make our way out of the apartment again.

"Whoa," Harper says, eyes going monstrous. The crush of bodies is too much for the narrow walkway. We can barely move. "This is *insane*. Is everyone in Italy going to this thing?"

"More like everyone in Europe," I say, but that's not exactly true. The families and children all seem to have gone home. The people on the streets are our age: students and teenagers, dressed in skimpy costumes, their faces painted with dark eyeliner and glitter.

Music vibrates through the air. I feel it before I hear it. It pulses up from the sidewalk, moving through my bones and humming over my skin. The heavy bass reaches my ears, and it sounds like a heartbeat.

*Bomp bomp bomp bomp.*

"You really think the red's okay?" Mara asks, linking arms with me. "I don't look like a whore?"

I smile at her sweetly and rest my head on her shoulder. "You look great. We all do."

We were right to go all out with our costumes. Everyone in the crowd is decked out in crazy masks and outfits: devil's horns twist out of heads, long snouts protrude from faces, and forked tails trail away from people's backs. Angel's wings glitter in the fading sunlight.

I catch Mara checking her reflection in the window of the butcher shop as the crowd carries us forward. I don't know what she's stressed about. Her lacy red teddy fits like a glove, showing off every curve of her tiny pixie body. Her eyes shift up to where the dead pig hangs behind the glass, empty eye sockets staring.

She winces. "That thing is so gross."

"The whole place was creepy." Harper drops her arms around our shoulders, inserting herself between us. She doesn't bother asking if we think she looks good. Her white teddy looks angelic and soft against her deeply tanned shoulders, and her sky-high heels show off her long legs. "What kind of person would ever want to work in a butcher shop?"

I think of the butcher girl—*Elyse*—and shiver. "No idea."

I check my reflection, too, just before we turn the corner. I'm wearing nude and black lace, devil's horns twisting out of my auburn hair. I pull at my jacket, feeling naked. The crowd and the people suddenly feel like too much. The food stands from earlier are gone, and now the smell of human bodies hangs heavy in the air. It's gotten dark, the sun no more than a thin gold line on the horizon. The last bits of light bounce off glittery angel's wings and sweaty arms.

The crowd surges forward, and we're tossed into the wide, open square. The beat drops, and the people around us scream, elbows and shoulders jabbing the soft parts of my body as they jump and gyrate.

They're so happy. Intensely, ecstatically happy. I feel my own lips curving to mimic theirs, that touch of nerves mostly vanishing.

*Tonight's going to be epic*, I tell myself. I look at Harper and Mara and see matching grins on their faces. Harper leans in close, cupping a hand around her mouth.

"Drinks!" she shouts.

I nod, and we push our way through the crowd to find the trattoria. Candlelight flickers, dancing over dark skin and black eyes. The light distorts everyone's features, making their teeth seem jagged, their eyes hooded and haunting. Horns curl away from their heads. Demon's horns. Devil's horns.

"Look," I say, spotting Giovanni by the fountain. He's wearing a devil's mask, too, but it's shoved up on his forehead so I can see his gorgeous face. I feel a grin pulling at my lips, and I start pushing through the crowd toward him, Harper and Mara following along behind me.

His eyes light up when he catches sight of me. "Bella!"

I stumble out of the crowd, and Giovanni sweeps me into his arms, practically lifting me off my feet. I feel myself squeal. I never act like this. Like I'm some grinning schoolgirl. I love it.

Giovanni puts me back down on the ground and turns to Mara and Harper, raising an eyebrow. "Are you going to introduce me to your beautiful friends, bella?"

"I'm Mara," Mara says. "I've been on your tour a couple of times. I don't know if you remember . . ."

"Ciao, Mara. Of course I remember you. You always asked the most fascinating questions." Giovanni plants a kiss on both cheeks. Mara blushes, deeply.

He turns to Harper. "And you must be Harper." He says her name like *Arpurr*, more purr than words. Harper smiles, wickedly, and offers him her hand.

"Pleasure," she says. Giovanni brushes her hand aside and kisses her on both cheeks.

"Were the costumes your idea?" he asks, raising his eyebrows appreciatively at our leather jackets and lingerie.

"They were Berkley's, actually," Harper admits.

"But you styled them," I point out, motioning to the fierce aviators she found in the accessories bin. Harper beams.

"*Sono perfetti,*" Giovanni says, squeezing her shoulder. Just as I'm about to get the teensiest bit jealous, he moves back to my side and presses a hand against my lower back, claiming me. Shivers race up my skin.

"You ladies need drinks," he says, and as though on cue, a tiny devil-headed man appears, carrying a plastic tray filled with neon-colored shots. Giovanni says something in Italian and unloads three shots from the tray, which he passes out to me and my friends. He winks.

"Cheers," he says.

I notice a group of girls huddled together as I throw back my shot. They kneel on the stone steps leading up to the piazza, dressed all in white, with lacy veils draped over their dark hair. Everywhere else is crowded with bodies, but the girls are at the center of a wide-open space. It's like no one wants go near them.

"What's their deal?" I ask Giovanni. Candlelight sends shadows dancing over the girls' faces. I can't see their eyes, but their lips seem to be moving together, reciting something.

Giovanni follows my gaze, frowning. "Them? They are no one."

"Are they *praying*?"

He rolls his eyes toward the sky and holds out his hands, like he's asking someone in the heavens for help. "*Yes*. They are always praying."

"But why? Don't they like the party?"

"It is not the party they do not like, bella. It is the people who come to the party."

"*Us?*" I must look hurt, because Giovanni laughs.

"Do not take it personally." He leans closer to me so that I can hear him over the pulsing music. "This town has many old families. They remember what it was like before all the tourists came. How it used to be quiet. Now there are college girls dancing in the piazza every night and college boys throwing up on the sidewalks. Some people think this is . . ." Giovanni pauses, searching for the word. "*Peccato* . . . sin?"

"Why would Cambria hold a festival like this if you think tourists are sinful?"

"Not all of us think like the old families. Tourists bring *money*. Cambria is a very poor place. Most of us, we like the rich Americans drinking at our trattorias."

I nudge him with my elbow. "And going on your walking tours?"

He laughs. "Yes, yes, exactly. You tourists pay for my school. To me you are sent from God."

He pulls his devil's mask down over his face and nods to a group of bedeviled strangers who've been gathering near the fountain. "Enjoy the drinks, my friends. The performance is about to start."

"Performance?" Mara shouts. Someone's turned up the music, and I barely hear her voice. "What performance?"

I shrug. Giovanni climbs onto the fountain, unbuttoning his shirt as he does. He's painted an inverted pentagram onto his chest in something that looks a hell of a lot like blood. The crowd whoops and cheers. He salutes and tosses his shirt over their heads. It hangs in the velvety night sky for a second, a ghostly white bird.

"We need a sacrifice!" he shouts, cupping his hands around his mouth so that his voice booms above the music. "Who among you is brave enough to volunteer?"

I look over at Harper and Mara, and the three of us burst into laughter. Meanwhile, more people have climbed onto the fountain with Giovanni, candlelight flashing over the blacks and reds and purples of their masks. The shadows make them look like they're moving.

They start removing their clothes, just like Giovanni did, and tossing T-shirts and tank tops into the crowd. They have strange symbols painted over their skin in the same bloody paint.

*"Sacrificio!"* they chant, their voices merging into one. *"Sacrificio!"*

A girl steps away from the crowd, and the people around her erupt into cheers. I feel a prickle of jealousy as Giovanni takes her by the hand and pulls her onto the fountain beside him. She makes quite a show out of opening her mouth and slowly sticking out her tongue.

"What's he giving her?" Mara shouts.

Giovanni places a small white pill on the girl's tongue. She swallows, and he turns her around. The crowd surges forward as she plummets backward, catching her before she can hit the ground. The people in front of us pump their hands in the sky, jumping up and down and cheering. For a moment I can't see anything, can't hear anything. I'm entirely surrounded by noise and energy and people. It's intoxicating.

"Another!" Giovanni shouts once the crowd has calmed down. His eyes find mine, and I feel my heart start thumping. He crooks a finger at me.

I don't know if it's the music pumping through my blood or if it's Giovanni's delicious smile, but suddenly all I want in the world is to be standing on that fountain next to him, closing my eyes as he places that white pill on my tongue. I start pushing my way through the people packed in around me.

"Are you serious?" Mara grabs me by the arm, jerking me back. "You're actually going up there?"

"You think that's a good idea?" Harper adds, twisting her fingers together. "I mean, this party is a lot like the one . . ." She swallows the rest of her sentence, then turns to Mara for help. "You know?"

"No," I deadpan, even though I know they must be talking about my panic episode. "I don't."

I shoulder through the crowd, and they part to let me through.

"*Sacrificio!*" they chant. "*Sacrificio!*"

I let their energy propel me forward until Mara and Harper's objections seem like silly, faraway things. Giovanni leans down and wraps his fingers around my arm, pulling me onto the fountain beside him. I stumble forward, catching myself before I get some of the "blood" smeared across his chest onto my dress.

"It's corn syrup," he tells me, pressing a finger into the pentagram. He lifts the blood to my mouth, and I wrap my lips around it, smearing the red over my cheek. It tastes sweet, like sugar.

Giovanni grins and leans closer to me. "I knew you'd be my sacrifice," he says in my ear, his voice making the words curl and dance.

"Always." I open my mouth, and he places the small white pill on my tongue.

I swallow.

# CHAPTER 14

*Before*

I'm humming. That's right, I'm actually *humming*, like a cartoon princess in a Disney movie. I half expect cockroaches and mice to crawl out of the walls and start braiding my hair.

I've never hummed inside the institute, and I'm unprepared for how my voice echoes off the concrete walls of my room, haunting and toneless, like part of the melody has seeped in between the cracks and gotten lost on its way back. As soon as this thought comes to me, I press my lips together, going quiet.

But even the eternal creepiness of this place can't make me feel bad—not today, day forty-two of my imprisonment. The last day of my sixth week. The day I'm finally getting out of here.

The thought makes me smile. I've got my suitcase propped on my bed, and I'm gleefully folding and packing what few possessions they let me bring here. T-shirts. Comb. The toiletries that don't contain any alcohol. An ugly stuffed hippopotamus my mom insisted I bring with me. I won it during a class trip to Coney Island in eighth grade, and it's lived in the back of my closet ever since, but Mom seemed to think it'll bring me some comfort. It only makes me think of Tayla, how I won it because she distracted the guy running the game, and he didn't notice me steal a few more balls . . .

I shake my head, pushing the memory aside. In just a few short hours, I'll be back in my bedroom, where the nail polish and good skin care and colorful clothes live. I'll be able to wear earrings again and listen to music and go online and text my friends. I can't wait to chill in Harper's dorm, like we did during my first semester at NYU, drinking the beer she got some older guy to buy for her and gossiping about her crush on her TA. And maybe Mara will let me borrow her notes from her first-year classes—or better yet, tutor me. If I bust my ass over the summer, I might be able to catch up with them before fall semester.

I'll even put this hippopotamus in the middle of my

bed if it'll make my mom happy. Who cares? At least I'll be home.

I've started to hum again when a hand drops onto my shoulder.

I screech and whirl around, flinging the hippopotamus across the floor.

Dr. Andrews picks it up. "Who's this guy?" she asks, gazing lovingly down at the animal's ugly stuffed head. Like it's a puppy.

I feel my face close in on itself. Something's wrong. She shouldn't be here. She doesn't *fit* here. Her white-on-beige-on-white ensemble belongs in her office, in the "nice" part of the institute, surrounded by white furniture and soft lighting and carefully chosen flowers. Nothing about her makes sense in this small, close room, with the crooked pipe jutting across the ceiling and the fluorescent light buzzing overhead.

Without realizing what I'm doing, I edge backward, colliding with the wall. "What do you want?"

Dr. Andrews places the hippopotamus on my bed and then sits down beside it, one hand still resting on its ugly purple head. "I was hoping we might talk for a bit. Sit down?"

I swallow. I don't want to talk for a bit, not when we've spent the last six weeks talking and now we're done and I'm cured. But her voice has a quiet power, one that I have a hard time disobeying.

I sit, mattress springs creaking beneath my legs. "What do you want to talk about?"

Dr. Andrews removes her hand from the hippo's head. She glances at my suitcase. "I've been thinking about the story you told during our last session. About Tayla?"

I blink. "It wasn't a story. It's what happened."

"I've looked into some of the details. Tayla was accepted to Connecticut College, not Columbia. And she only made JV in volleyball, not varsity."

I shrug, trying for casual. "I guess I mixed some of the details up. Does that really matter?"

Dr. Andrews fixes me with a calm gaze. "You lied to me, Berkley."

I can hear my heart beating in my ears, a steady hum. *They catch you in a lie and you're totally fucked.*

"I didn't lie," I say, trying to keep my voice steady. "Tayla was really intense, just like I told you. That thing with the test—that actually happened."

I can still remember her crumpling that test up in one hand, throwing it across the hall in frustration. I told her to chill out—it was *one* test—and she rounded on me, furious, shouting about how some people care about more than parties and gossip.

I shake the memory from my head. "I just changed some of the details to help you understand—that's all."

Dr. Andrews's expression doesn't change. "Is that so?"

"Cross my heart."

She straightens a wrinkle in her pants and then folds her hands in her lap. "I'm afraid I think there's more to it than that. I know the plan was for you to head home after six weeks here, but I feel strongly, as do my supervisors, that we need to address the underlying issues that caused you to lie before we can recommend releasing you."

I replay what she just said, but the words lose their meaning before they manage to sink into my brain. "What? What does that mean?"

"It means I'm recommending we . . ." Dr. Andrews swallows, and her eyes flit to the door of my dorm room, almost like she's expecting someone else to waltz in and help her out. "I'm recommending that we keep you here for a few more weeks. So we can dig down into the reason you don't want to tell me about what happened with Tayla."

*A few more weeks.*

A jittery feeling starts in my gut, like when you've just realized you're the butt of a joke but you haven't heard the punch line yet. I force my lips to curve, not quite a smile.

"I can't stay here for a few more weeks," I say. "I'm going home today."

Dr. Andrews tilts her head, sympathetic. "Berkley . . ."

Whatever else she says gets lost beneath the low hum that's started at the back of my head. "I can't stay here for a few more weeks," I say again, urgently. "I'm going home *today*. I've already started packing."

I jerk my chin at my suitcase. It seems sad, suddenly. Just a few folded T-shirts and bundled-up socks. It reminds me of being a little kid, pretending I was going to run away from home whenever my parents were mean to me.

"Berkley, listen to me—"

"No!" My voice comes out louder than I intended. My vision flickers, then sparks back to life, the colors sharper than they were a moment ago. The room seems to sway. I blink a few times, trying to regain my bearings.

Dr. Andrews doesn't look serene anymore. Her eyebrows form harsh angles in the middle of her forehead. Her nostrils flare.

"Berkley," she says, voice hard. "Please sit down."

"I *am* sitting." But that's not true. I'm standing, and I have the ugly hippo clutched in my hands so tightly that my knuckles ache. I blink again, trying to remember the last few seconds. Everything feels hazy. Even the colors in the room seem weird, like I'm looking out through tinted glass.

"Sit down, and we'll talk this through." Dr. Andrews stands slowly, and she has her hands out in front of her like I'm a wild animal that she needs to approach with caution.

The haziness fades as fury moves through me. She's

acting like *I'm* the problem here just because I don't want
to be locked up inside this cold, concrete room for who
knows how long.

I squeeze the hippo tighter. This is all backward. I'm
not crazy. She's the one being crazy.

"I won't stay here!" I feel my voice rise, like it's a phys-
ical thing with sharp nails, climbing up the back of my
throat. "You can't keep me. I'm only supposed to be here
for six weeks. Six weeks!"

Dr. Andrews unclips something small and black from
her waist and holds it to her mouth—a walkie-talkie.
"This is Dr. Andrews. We have a code five in Block C. I
repeat, we have a code five—"

I throw the hippo, and it bounces off Dr. Andrews's
head, mussing her hair and knocking the walkie-talkie
from her hand. The hunk of black plastic hits the floor
with a *smack*.

Dr. Andrews presses her lips into a thin line, fixing
her hair with a jerk of her hand. "You're making this
much harder on yourself than it needs to be."

"You can't do this." My voice trembles. "You can't keep
me here."

Dr. Andrews doesn't answer. She doesn't have to. I
can already hear the echo of footsteps pounding down
the hallway. They're coming for me.

I back up against the wall, pressing my whole body

against the cold concrete blocks. They're going to take me away, take me somewhere even worse than this small, cold cell. I start shaking my head. The word *no* runs on repeat through my brain.

*Nononononononono.*

Dr. Andrews steps aside as a large male nurse bursts into my room. I look around for something to throw at him, to keep him away, but all my possessions are already inside my suitcase, packed and ready to take home.

I pick up the entire suitcase and hurl it across the room. It hits the nurse square in the chest, making a satisfying *thwunk*. He staggers back, stumbling into the door.

Another nurse appears behind him, a woman this time. She holds a needle.

"Calm down, darling," she coos, easing past the doubled-over male nurse. The tip of her needle looks sharp beneath the flickering fluorescent lights. "This is just a little something to help you relax."

I shake my head, pressing harder into the wall behind me. I've seen the girls who've gotten "a little something" like this before. They walk around like broken dolls, eyes glassy, feet heavy. They drool while they watch television.

The nurse advances on me. I look around for

something to throw, but everything I brought with me is heaped on the floor, trapped beneath my suitcase. Dr. Andrews and the male nurse form a barricade in front of my door. I'm backed against a wall with nowhere to run, no way to fight.

I think of those poor, glassy-eyed girls. I don't want to be one of those girls.

I start to scream. I scream until tears spring to my eyes and my throat feels raw. The female nurse grabs me roughly. I swing out with one hand, and the male nurse charges forward and pushes me against the wall as the woman jabs the needle into the fleshy part of my arm. Metal slides through my skin. Tears spring to my eyes, and a warm, heavy feeling moves through me. My eyelids grow heavy . . .

The nurses shift to the side, parting just long enough for me to catch sight of Dr. Andrews hovering behind them. She's watching me with an impassive look on her face.

"Go to sleep, Berkley," she says. "We'll talk about this tomorrow."

*And the day after that*, I think, as the darkness falls over me. *And the day after that, and after that, and . . .*

# CHAPTER 15

## *After*

I experience the next few hours in flashes.

*Flash*: sweaty people, fists pumping, too-sharp teeth gleaming.

*Flash*: twisted rubber, snarling devil's masks, drooping eyeholes.

*Flash*: makeup running down faces in streaks.

Harper and Mara dance beside me. Their hands are on my shoulders, spinning me in fast circles that send me careening into the people around us. They wiggle their hips, and their mouths twist, laughing and shouting.

They open their hands, and small white pills appear on their palms. We place them on our tongues and toast with champagne. "You're only young once!" and then the bubbles chase the pills down our throats.

I take a sharp inhale, and oxygen burns up my lungs. Cold air nips the back of my neck as bodies press in around me, sweat rolling down bare skin.

And then they're gone, and Giovanni is in front of me. He flashes me a smile filled with brilliant white teeth. He drops his arms around my shoulders, pressing his hips into mine.

"Bella," he whispers. He says it again and again, his voice tangling and echoing in my head. *Bella bella bella bella . . .*

*This is what it's like to be free,* I think. I feel the smile in my mouth and cheeks, and then it stretches through my whole body, filling me like sunshine. Giovanni tastes like ice and cigarettes. The air smells like sweat.

It's all I've ever wanted.

Hours or minutes later, a girl separates from the crowd and makes her way over to me. I try to focus on her, but she blurs into the night. My head pounds.

She's dressed like an angel, all in white, her dark hair a shocking contrast to the lace veil draped over it. Her features seem familiar, but they don't add up to anything in my head.

I turn to ask Giovanni if he knows her. But Giovanni isn't there. The people dancing around me are strangers.

The girl is beside me now. She says something, and

the words seem to float in front of her mouth, like a thought bubble in a comic.

"Do you want to dance?"

The music throbs in my ears, making my head spin. "Where's Giovanni?"

The girl puts her arms around my waist. She leans in close to me, her lips brushing against my earlobe, as she says, "He went to get us more wine, remember? Come, dance."

My body starts to move, obeying her command before my mind has a chance to think it over. Bleary questions form in the back of my head, never quite coming into focus.

*Why did . . . ?*

*Didn't Mara and Harper . . . ?*

*Who is . . . ?*

I blink, slowly. I can't remember anything that happened in the last few hours, but I feel the lost time in the arches of my feet. They ache, like they always do when I've been wearing heels all night. I feel suddenly dizzy.

I sway, but the girl holds me around the waist, pulling me upright again. Her hands are strong.

She's a good dancer. Her hips swing with the music. Her skin is soft. She moves her hands down my waist, pulling me closer. She smells like perfume. Something heavy and floral.

No, not perfume. *Incense.*

Something stirs in the back of my mind—*this isn't, she isn't, don't*—but the thought breaks apart before I can grasp hold of it.

"I should go," I murmur. The music pulses, swallowing my voice. The ground tilts beneath me. I try again. "I should go home."

I bring one hand to my forehead, squinting into the candlelight. Sweat gathers on my palms, and I taste something sour at the back of my throat. I blink into the crowd, trying to find someone I know.

The faces around me are so strange. The candlelight distorts everyone's features, turning their teeth jagged, their eyes hooded and haunting. Horns curl away from their heads. They look like demon's horns.

And now the piazza is spinning. I squeeze my eyes shut and then force them open again. My eyelids feel heavier than they're supposed to. I turn in a slow circle, searching the shadowy crowd for Mara's blond pixie cut or Harper's long legs.

"Have you seen my friends?" I ask the girl in white.

Her eyebrows go up. "Your friends are with us, bella, remember?" She holds me steady, her fingers light on my hips. "We are having a private party."

My head swims. "I need . . . Harper . . ."

"Yes, come on. I will bring you to her." She places a hand on my back and steers me away from the dancers.

I press my palm to my leg to steady myself. There's a sweaty handprint glistening on my skin when I move it.

As soon as we leave the crowd, the air around us seems to still, like the city is holding its breath. We step out of the main piazza and down a narrow alley. It reeks of smoke—cigarettes and something else. Something earthier.

I blink a few times to allow my eyes to adjust to the dark. Gray bricks rise around me, and abandoned devil's masks stare from the shadows. Empty Solo cups roll along the sidewalks, spilling something pink onto the cobblestones.

My tongue feels thick. "Where are we going?"

"Only a little farther." The angel squeezes my arm. "And then you will see your friends."

I frown down at my feet. My shoes are gone. One of my toenails has been torn in half, and blood bubbles beneath the remaining ragged edge.

"What's your name?" My words blur together. *Wasyername?*

"I am Angelica. You don't remember me?"

I narrow my eyes to slits, studying the angel's dark face and full lips. I do remember her, but it takes me a long moment to work out why.

"You were in the church," I say finally, remembering

her long, thin face and huge eyes. The locks of dark hair hanging down her back. "We lit a candle."

She pats my arm. "Yes, yes. We said a prayer for your ankle."

"I remember." I cross my arms over my chest, hands damp and shaking. Something else is bothering me, but I can't put my finger on what it is. There's a prickle in the air, like the sharp edge of a knife. Something's wrong.

A wolf whistle echoes from the piazza. The sound bounces off the cobblestones, chasing after us.

Something frightened me back at the festival. It was a bone-deep fear, like instinct. The same way animals know to run from predators. I blink, slowly, trying to remember. My thoughts are soupy and slow.

Angelica's veil flashes white in the darkness. I lift a hand, fingers grazing the lace. "What's this?"

"It is called a *mantiglia*. It's to cover your hair in church."

Church. Incense.

The memory comes to me in a flash: three girls huddling on the steps of the piazza, their lips moving together in prayer. Giovanni rolling his eyes at them.

*It is not the party they do not like, bella. It is the people who come to the party.*

"You were with those girls," I murmur. "Those praying girls."

My heart starts beating faster. The smell of sweat in the air is stronger somehow. Ripe and nauseating. I pull my arm away from Angelica and stumble backward, my bad ankle twisting. Fresh pain beats beneath my skin like a pulse.

Angelica frowns. "*Scusa?* What is wrong?"

My mind works in slow motion, trying to put the puzzle together. I think of spiky letters on my bedsheets, written in blood. *It is the people who come to the party.*

I feel a shift behind my shoulder—a shadow moving—and whip around. There's no one there.

"You don't like us," I say, turning back around. It sounds silly when I put it like this. Something a child would say. I swallow and add, "Giovanni said."

Angelica's lips split into a smile. I blink, the dazzle of it too much to take. "Giovanni told you this? How would he know?"

"He says you don't like tourists."

"Of course we like you. We are throwing a party for you. Come, come."

Angelica stops at the end of the alleyway and crooks a finger, beckoning me to follow her around the corner.

The drugs have started to wear off, leaving my head pounding and raw. I can't tell if the fear is real or if it's a side effect of the chemicals fighting with my brain. The moonlight feels like fingernails dragging over my skin. The air is feverish, cold and hot at the same time. I shouldn't have wandered off with this strange girl.

*But she's not strange,* I think. *She said a prayer for me.*

Angelica rounds the corner. I turn, looking back the way we came. The party feels far away now, a distant tangle of laughter and music and sweat. I'll never find my way back through the maze of sidewalks.

"Wait." I take a step after Angelica, cringing when my toe comes down on something sharp. "Wait, please. I don't know how to get back."

The alley appears empty. I walk past a dumpster, and a stray cat darts out in front of me, a streak of matted gray fur. I stumble backward, swearing. The cat stops directly in front of me and hisses, teeth flashing, spit flying from its lips. A second later, it disappears beneath another dumpster.

A voice says, from behind me, "Ciao."

I whip around. The bartender with the green hair and tattoos stands at the mouth of the alley. *Francesca.* Her lips curl at the corner. Half smile, half smirk.

"What are you doing here?"

Francesca lifts her chin a fraction of an inch. The smirking smile doesn't leave her face. "We are throwing a party for you. Didn't Angelica tell you?

I blink, and her outfit leaps out at me: white dress, white veil. She isn't close enough to know for sure, but I feel certain her hair smells like incense.

"What party?"

Francesca tilts her head to the side, the movement almost catlike. "Come, and I will show you."

She takes a step toward me, and I back up, slamming into the dumpsters. Her smirk widens.

The air feels strange. Boiling. I feel it on every inch of my skin. I say, "I want to go home."

"Ah, but we cannot let you do that."

Two others girls appear from nowhere—Angelica and the girl from the butcher shop, Elyse. I'd forgotten how tall she was. She towers over us all.

They stand on either side of Francesca, blocking my only path out. The lace covering their hair makes them look soft and pious. Like angels.

My lungs clench, and I feel my heart working inside my chest, beating so hard it hurts. "What do you want?"

Francesca nods at her friends, and the two girls move forward, each of them grabbing one of my arms. Blood rushes into my head fast, leaving me dizzy. It doesn't occur to me to scream until a beat too late, and by that time, Angelica has a hand pressed over my lips.

"Shh . . ." she murmurs through my muffled cries. "It is okay. You are sick. We are going to say a prayer for you. To help you."

*Crazy*, I think. I let my arms and legs go limp so I'll be harder to hold, but the girls grip tight, refusing to let me fall. They're stronger than I am, their arms lean and muscular beneath browned skin and white lace. They easily twist my hands behind my back, half leading, half dragging me out of the alley. A rusted Fiat waits at the corner, trunk already popped and waiting.

*No way.* I dig my heels into the ground, thrusting the weight of my body back to keep them from pulling me farther. Why is this happening to me? After the institute and everything else?

Why does this always happen to *me*?

I twist my face away from Angelica. "Help! Someone please help me!"

Francesca says something in Italian. Elyse shakes me—*hard*—and Angelica grabs for my mouth, whispering that I need to be quiet.

"Don't make us gag you," Elyse hisses into my ear.

She twists my wrist behind my back, sending pain shooting through my arm and forcing me forward. The car's trunk yawns before me, dark and ominous. Fear squeezes the air from my lungs.

I've heard stories about American girls traveling through Europe before. How they're sometimes taken by big men with Russian accents and greasy muscles, hidden away in cramped rooms with sagging mattresses, drugged until they're submissive enough for the men to do whatever they want to them.

But these girls look normal. They work in butcher shops and bars. They're girls I might've been friends with.

A hand grabs the back of my neck, fingers pressing into the base of my skull. Someone kicks the backs of my legs, and my knees buckle. From there, it's easy for them to wrestle me into the car. My shins bang into the rusted bumper, and my elbow snaps against the side of the trunk, pain flickering up bones and skin.

I try to fight, but there are three sets of hands pushing me forward, holding me in place. I lose my balance and fall, my face slamming into the oily fabric of the car's trunk. The air is hot and close.

I roll over, but the space is cramped. By the time I'm on my back and trying to sit up, Francesca is already lowering the trunk door.

"Why are you doing this?" I shout.

"Because you are *diavolina*." She pushes the word through clenched teeth, her mouth a snarl. "You are what is wrong with this village."

She snickers and lets the door fall closed, leaving me alone in the dark.

# CHAPTER 16

*O*<sup>h</sup> *God.*

I claw at the underside of the trunk door, looking for a latch or an opening—*anything*. But my hands tremble so badly I'm not sure I could work one if I found it.

Voices rise and fall outside the car. I press my lips together, trying to calm my shaky breathing so I can hear what they're saying.

The voices fall silent. Car doors slam open and closed, and the Fiat shifts as people climb inside. We begin to move. I dig my fingers into the oily bottom of the trunk. Everything in my body—from the tiny muscles around the corners of my mouth, to my calves, even my toes—tightens.

The cobblestone roads are rough beneath the Fiat's bald tires. I feel each pebble jolt through me. Each turn sends me tumbling into the side of the car. Before long, my bones ache and my skin feels tender and bruised. My head spins.

I can't help being reminded of the twisty roads I sped along on Giovanni's moped, how they corkscrewed in and around themselves in sharp curls and breakneck turns. I press my lips together and focus on my breathing to keep myself from being sick.

I'm not claustrophobic—not technically. But the small, enclosed space makes me feel trapped. I flash back to the institute—*hard mattress and concrete walls and stiff restraints holding me down*—and cold fear runs through my veins.

After what feels like a long time, the car stops. I'm so motion sick that I don't realize we aren't moving until I hear the creak of a door opening. I push my body to the very back of the trunk, my breathing suddenly shaky. Pins and needles tiptoe up my legs.

Footsteps scrape against cobblestones. Pebbles skid across the ground. There's a creak of metal, and dim light pours into the trunk. I blink into it, squinting. Three shadows take shape above me.

"Get up," Francesca says, her voice flat. I think of the cool bartender who gave me free shots my first night, the girl working Professor Coletti's dinner party.

The Francesca that's standing over me seems like a different person: hard and angry and emotionless. I'm afraid of her.

When I don't move, she grabs me by the arm and drags me out. I stumble to the ground, my knee scraping against a rock. I cringe, looking around desperately as I struggle to stand.

Elyse grabs me and twists my arms behind my back, grinning savagely when I cringe with pain. Angelica covers my mouth with one hand, but I notice that she does this gently, like she feels bad about it. Her hands are soft and smell like lavender soap.

"Quiet," she murmurs. "We're almost there."

I look around, wildly. We're parked outside the church where I sprained my ankle, only a few blocks from Harper and Mara's apartment. I might even be able to find my way back, if I get a head start.

Without thinking, I bite down on Angelica's hand. Skin breaks beneath my teeth, and something salty and metallic bursts over my tongue. *Blood.* The hand jerks away from me, and Angelica mutters something in Italian.

"Help me!" I scream. My voice is hoarse and ragged. I try to wiggle away from Elyse, but she's too strong. "Please, somebody! Help me—"

Pain explodes across my cheekbone. My face whips to the side, the nerves along my neck flaring. The air leaves my lungs in an involuntary gasp.

Elyse *punched* me.

I blink a few times, but my vision's gone blurry. Everything seems to be spinning. I stretch out my jaw, tears springing to my eyes.

Elyse pushes me forward, and I move without protest, too shocked by the punch to put up a fight.

"Why are you doing this?" I gasp. The pain in my cheek dulls to a low pulse, and I feel it more in my bones than in my skin. "What do you want?"

Francesca studies me. The shadows make her nose longer, her eyebrows heavier. I can barely make out the green streaks in her dark hair.

If anyone here looks like a *diavolina*, it's her, not me.

She says, "I am Giovanni's girlfriend."

Understanding hits me like a slap. I remember how he sat at the trattoria, talking to her the night we met. How he just showed up at the party where she was working. *This is a small town*, he'd told me.

I say, tripping over the words, "He never told me he had a girlfriend, I swear."

Francesca tilts her head, considering me through the thick fan of her dark lashes. She's beautiful. It's intense, the kind of beauty that smacks you in the face and won't let you look away.

"We are meant to be together," she says casually. Her accent isn't as thick as Giovanni's, but it's there, smoothing the edges of her words and turning her *r*'s to velvet.

"Slutty tourists like you distract him for the summer, but he always comes back to me in the end."

I swallow and look into the faces of her two friends. "I won't go near him again, okay? I promise. Just let me go."

The girls look at each other. For a second, I think this might be over. They already took me on a joyride in the trunk of their fucking car. They have to realize that's enough to scare anyone away from some guy.

Francesca turns back to me and licks her lips. "I already told you. You are *diavolina*."

The word sends a chill down my spine. "Is that what you call sluts around here?"

"You must pay for your sins," Angelica says, her high bird voice sounding almost nervous. She tilts her head to the side, lips on the verge of a smile. "You are lucky we are here to help you."

Elyse snorts. "Yeah. Lucky."

"Let *go*," I shout as Elyse grabs for my arms. I back up against the car, jerking away from her. "This is *insane*. You're going to beat me up over a few kisses? I already told you I'd stay away from him!"

"*Quiet*," Elyse snaps. She twists my arm behind my back, sending pain flaring through my joints. "Do not make me punch you again."

She pushes, and I lurch forward, cringing. Angelica falls in line beside us, that eerie almost-smile still plastered across her face. I notice that she's humming, lightly, beneath her breath.

I press my eyes closed, fighting against the tears threatening to spill onto my cheeks. The feeling inside me is a low, static buzz. Pure adrenaline. It's the only thing keeping me from completely freaking out.

*This will be over soon,* I tell myself. They'll get bored of slapping me around soon enough. I just need to stay calm.

Angelica brushes a sweaty lock of hair out of my face and says, *"Aiutati che Dio t'aiuta."*

She draws a cross between my eyebrows with her thumb. Like she's giving me a blessing.

They don't take me inside the church. Instead, they lead me through a small, overgrown courtyard to the side of the building. Stone archways block out the sky, and weeds grow past my knees.

I focus on the adrenaline buzzing through me to keep from falling apart. "Where are we going?"

"It's a surprise," Francesca says. There's a hole in the wall at the side of the church. The grass in front is trampled flat, and someone has placed a few wooden boards over the jagged bricks along the ground.

Elyse lets go of my wrist. "Go," she says, jerking her chin at the hole.

I curl my arms protectively around my chest. Through

the hole, I see only yawning black darkness. I think of the catacombs Giovanni showed me: wall after wall of yellowed skulls, empty eye sockets staring out, teeth bared in matching grimaces. I shake my head. *No way in hell.*

A slice of a laugh. Elyse says, her voice booming, "You think you have a choice, *diavolina?*"

Two hands slam into my back. I hit the ground knees-first, smashing into packed dirt instead of cobblestones. I lurch forward, digging my fingers into the earth to keep them from trembling. Angelica says something in a high, panicky voice while Elyse and Francesca laugh terribly.

I should run. Get the hell out of here, while they're distracted. My eyes twitch from side to side, but it's too dark here to see anything. The ground slopes downward, and I can feel walls pressing in around me. The air feels thin and close.

A foot nudges my shoulder. "Get up."

I don't know what's down there, in the darkness, but Francesca and her friends stand behind me, blocking the only other way out. I push myself to my feet and take a tentative step forward.

*Stay calm*, I think, like a mantra. *This will be over soon.*

But I can't help the desperate thought that runs through my mind on repeat. *Why me? Why is it always, always me?*

There's nowhere for me to run. Nowhere to go. One by one, Francesca, Elyse, and Angelica climb into the hole after me. Together, the four of us make our way underground.

The tunnel twists and dips until, finally, I see candlelight sparking in the darkness, flames like trembling wings. Something about it makes me feel deeply uncomfortable.

*They've been planning this.*

The candles illuminate an arched doorway. Packed dirt falls away in clumps to reveal ancient rock walls below. My breath catches in my throat. Someone built a room down here, deep below the church. I make out the edges of hulking shapes beyond the doorway. Gold light dancing over flashing metal and dark wood and leather.

I stop walking, focusing on the static spikes of adrenaline shooting through my veins. I don't want to go into that room. I don't want to find out what those shapes are.

A jab in my back. *"Move."*

I slide my foot forward even as everything in my body screams not to. There's nowhere to go but in.

We move through the arched doorway, and the underground room comes into clearer focus. I notice the crosses first. There are dozens of them nailed to the walls, some gold and gleaming in the candlelight, others crude, no more than two pieces of wood roughly nailed together, and still others are intricate and polished to a deep shine.

They make the small space feel hot and airless, the walls boiling with hidden power.

My knees buckle—I almost fall—but Elyse yanks me up with a hard jerk on my arms.

The room isn't big, maybe ten or twelve feet square, with a low ceiling. The walls themselves look ancient beneath the crosses: brick covered in layers of dirt, patches of paint gone brown near the ceiling and doors. Thick white candles have been lined up around the edges of the walls.

I should try to escape. Elyse's grip has loosened since we got underground. If I pulled away now, I could catch her off guard. Shove Angelica aside, reach the tunnel, and race back up to the street. Scream for help.

The image is clear in my mind, so real that I can almost feel Elyse's hands falling away from my wrists, the kick of adrenaline as I push Angelica to the floor. I curl my toes into the dirt, calf muscles tensing.

But I can't make myself do it. The drugs—or the fear—have left me paralyzed, weak. Exhaustion seeps into my muscles, freezing me in place. I let Elyse push me the rest of the way into the room, cursing myself for being so weak.

"These rooms weren't discovered until the eighties." Francesca is saying. "Father Nicola thinks they were used during the Inquisition."

I see something dark move at the corner of my eye

and whip around, but it's only the shadows moving in the candlelight. Elyse snickers, cruelly.

"Dumb American slut," she mutters.

"Don't be mean," Angelica whispers, shooting her a look. "We're here to help her, remember?"

A cruel twist curls the corner of Elyse's mouth. "I remember why we're here."

I feel the hair lift off the back of my neck. *Help.* It's clear that word means something different to Elyse than it does to Angelica.

I look around the room, trying to figure out what type of "help" they plan to give me. There are only three pieces of furniture in the room: a chair with a leather seat, a long wooden table attached to some sort of lever, and a tall stool holding a stone object shaped like a small pyramid.

A shiver moves through me. "What was it for?"

"Torture," says Francesca, deadpan.

"This room is called the Tribunal of Inquisition," Angelica says in a delighted whisper. Her dark eyes twitch back to Francesca, like she's asking for permission to continue. Francesca nods, and Angelica adds, "It is where they put heretics on trial."

She finds a canvas backpack slumped next to the door and reaches inside, removing a battered black book. The spine reads *La Sacra Bibbia.* The Holy Bible, I translate.

I taste acid at the back of my throat, that same intense beat of fear I felt back at the festival when I realized Angelica smelled like incense. I find some last store of energy deep inside and jerk away from Elyse.

She swears in Italian and lunges for the exit. The energy drains out of me as quickly as it came. Seeing no other option, I push my body up against the wall, as far from Elyse as I can get. Candles flicker next to my feet, but at least I feel a little safer with my back against something solid. Elyse laughs, the sound sharp and sudden as a bark.

"You actually think there's a chance for you to get away?" She blocks the exit with her body, something dark flashing through her eyes. "Go on. *Try* it."

"Stop," Francesca snaps. "This isn't a game. We're not chasing her through the tunnels. We have work to do."

A flash of anger darts across Elyse's face; she looks like she's been denied a treat.

Angelica lowers her arm, and the backpack slides to the floor at her feet, upsetting a small cloud of dust. "I have been practicing," she says, casting a shy glance my way. "I am almost as good as a real priest now."

I'm still looking at the chair on the far side of the room. Restraints hang from the armrests. Thick leather ones.

Mouth dry, I ask, "Practicing what?"

"Some of us think you deserve a chance to repent." Francesca's voice twists around the word *some*—making it clear that it doesn't refer to her—and glances at Angelica. "Even if you are *diavolina*."

Angelica's shoulders have gone stiff. She says, staring down at the Bible, "*All* God's creatures deserve a chance to repent."

Francesca and Elyse share a smirk behind Angelica's back. Francesca says, "Of course they do."

I don't like the way they're talking. *Repent* and *God's creatures* and *priest*. I dig my fingers into the cracks between the stones, my arms weak and shaky. Heat rises up from the candles, but it feels like it's coming off the crosses. Like the crosses are burning me.

"What do you mean, *repent*?" My tongue feels thick and clumsy in my mouth.

Francesca lifts her chin. "No more questions."

She kneels beside the backpack and removes a small glass bottle with a white cross etched on the front. *Holy water.*

My eyes move over the room, landing on a rope attached to the ceiling via pulley, one looped end pooled on the ground near the stool holding the stone pyramid. I shiver, hard, like a cat, and avert my eyes before I can think about how those objects might've been used during the Inquisition. How they might be used on me now.

The sharp tip of the pyramid looks shinier than anything else down here. Like it's been polished.

"Elyse," Francesca says, her black eyes still on me. "Get her on her knees."

"Kneel," Elyse says, sounding bored.

I press myself further into the wall. It starts to crumble beneath my weight, chunks of dirt sticking to my sweat in patches.

Elyse's small white teeth flash between her lips. It's a small movement, just a twitch of her mouth, and I'm reminded of a dog looking at its prey. She grabs me by the shoulders and jerks my body down, slamming her knee into my stomach.

My internal organs seem to shift, making room for Elyse's bone and muscle. All the breath leaves my body in a gasp of air, and my eyesight blinks out, like someone flipped a switch. Pain rolls over me, thick like nausea.

I double over. Sink to my knees.

"Better," Elyse says. She doesn't sound bored anymore. Now she sounds excited.

I grit my teeth, forcing myself to breathe through the hurt. After a moment, I'm able to lift my head.

Angelica is staring, expression horrified. For a second, I think she's going to step in, *do* something, but then her free hand flutters up near her hair, anxiously adjusting her veil. "Should I begin?"

Francesca nods. "We are ready."

She'd been standing farther away from the other two, letting them do her dirty work while she watched, but now she moves closer. I hear her uncork the holy water with a *pop*.

Angelica holds up the Bible, letting it fall open to a page near the middle. She clears her throat. *"Exsúrgat Deus et dissipéntur inimíci ejus,"* she recites in a voice clear and high as a bell, *"et fúgiant qui odérunt eum a fácie ejus."*

I let my head drop, still gasping for breath. My insides feel bruised. Every inhale burns. I press a hand to my stomach, cringing.

Something cold and wet hits the top of my head, and I give an involuntary flinch.

"Have you heard the story of our Lucia?" I see the pointed toe of Francesca's leather flats slide closer. A moment later, she crouches in the dirt.

I swallow, trying to remember the story Giovanni told me. "She was a girl," I choke out. "A sacrifice."

Francesca lifts my chin with her finger, eyes searching my face. Behind her, Angelica continues reading.

*"Sicut déficit fumus defíciant; sicut fluit cera a fácie ígnis."*

"Long ago, Cambria was a very poor place. Our crops would not grow. Our wells ran dry." Francesca taps her temple with one finger. "But our priests were smart men. They realized that the townspeople were sinners and that was why God cursed us. So they chose a girl to be made into an example. A *diavolina*. One who is possessed.

"Lucia was chosen because she was always sleeping with new men and because she was not a believer, like us. After she died, the town became good again. It rained. Crops grew. The priests, they thought if just one demon was exorcised, the others would follow. They were right."

Francesca lifts her eyes to mine and smiles. For a moment I'm reminded of the girl with the Lucky Charms tattoos and wicked smile, the girl I could imagine being friends with. She seemed so normal, not like Angelica, pious to the point of madness, or Elyse, who seems to actually *like* causing pain.

I gasp, *"Please . . .* why are you doing this?"

Francesca says, "We think now it is the same. If we perform an exorcism on one slutty American girl, the other slutty American girls will all leave, too. Just like Lucia."

Somewhere deep inside me, something begins to hum. I feel it vibrating in my palms and at the base of my spine. I jerk my head from side to side, looking at the chair with the leather restraints, and the sharp stone pyramid, and the table. Panic rattles up my chest.

They didn't bring me down here to hit me a few times, scare me away from their boyfriends.

They brought me here to sacrifice me.

I dig my fingers into the dirt, focusing on the hard press of earth beneath my fingernails. "You're crazy," I spit. A glob of saliva lands on the dirt between my fingers. "All of you. You're *sick*."

Francesca's lip curls. "We will see who is sick."

# CHAPTER 17

*Before*

B learily, I open my eyes.

Plaster stretches above me, cracked and discolored from years of water damage. It's not the ceiling in my dorm room—I notice that right away. The cracks are different from the ones I've memorized over the last six weeks. Unfamiliar.

I turn my head to the side, releasing a groan. This small movement feels impossibly difficult. The room looks like my dorm room, except there's only one bed and no windows. None of my stuff is here. I'm alone, lying on my back.

I try to turn, to study the rest of the space, but I'm still under sedation. My head feels too heavy, the muscles in my neck not strong enough to lift it. I try to push myself to a sitting position, but thick fabric cuts into my wrists and chest, holding me. Restraints.

*I was in solitary for a month*, I remember Sofia telling me. That must be what this is. They've deemed me too crazy for the crazy house, so they dumped me here.

Just a few hours ago, I thought I was going home.

Tears form in my eyes, but I blink them away. I want to be unconscious again, to drift back to whatever drug-induced dream world I was in before. Anywhere is better than this strange, empty room.

I clench my eyes shut—tight—and wait to fall back asleep.

You don't spend a lot of time awake when you're this medicated. I learn this over the next few days, in the brief moments when I'm able to keep my eyes open for more than a minute or two.

Tayla and I got mono in seventh grade, one after the other. The doctor thought we both caught it by drinking from the same soda bottle. That was the only other time in my life when I've spent full days in bed, too tired to lift my head, staring up at the ceiling. Only then, I had Tayla going through it with me. We'd FaceTime when we were both awake for more than a couple of minutes, tell each other about all the dumb things we'd dreamed, complain about how boring it was to be sick, or wonder whether Jackson Phillips (our mutual crush) noticed that we weren't in school. When we started feeling better, we'd watch the same crap TV—her in her bed, me in my own, phones pressed to our ears so we could hear each other laugh.

There's no one with me in this cold, dark room. Tayla is dead and gone. The flickering overhead hurts my eyes. The voices echoing from the hallway make my head pound. Those are the worst parts—when I'm awake.

Sleep is a luxury. Black and dreamless.

They remove the restraints from my wrists after twenty-four hours, but I'm not allowed into the cafeteria or any of the other public areas. Food is brought to me on a cold metal tray, and I don't know what it is, exactly, only that it tastes like mush and I have to work hard to keep it down. My mom used to make me pancakes when I felt sick. Waffles. French toast drenched in real syrup. She'd make faces with berries and whipped cream. The medicine makes my mouth feel numb. I don't even know if I'd be able to taste the sugar in the syrup.

If I don't eat everything, the nurse who comes to collect our plates and utensils gives me a dirty look before scurrying away.

"They make a note of your appetite in your chart," she warns me after breakfast on the second day, when I barely touch the soft, sludgy food they served me. "Not eating is a sign of passive aggression."

I knew that. I feel stupid for forgetting.

After that, I lick my tray clean every meal.

I'm released after three days (has it only been three days? It felt like weeks and weeks). They've lowered my meds, but I still feel like my head is filled with packing peanuts. The tips of my fingers tingle.

My canvas slip-ons scuff over the concrete floors in the hallway. *Scuff. Scuff.* The sound makes me think of zombies stumbling around on half-dead limbs, their hands grasping in front of them. I walk past Lara sobbing in the corner. And Genie, who winds a lock of brown hair around her finger and pulls. A cockroach climbs up the wall behind her, disappearing through a crack in the plaster.

The hall leading to my room feels ten degrees too cold. Goose bumps crawl up my arms, making the tiny brown hairs stand straight up, like soldiers called to attention. I stop outside my room, but I don't open the door.

I don't want to face that room. I don't want to see that someone's unpacked my suitcase, placing all my things back where they belong. T-shirts folded and tucked inside dresser drawers. That ugly hippopotamus sitting in the middle of my bed.

But it's not like I have a choice. I take a deep breath. Turn the doorknob.

Sofia looks up from the book she'd been reading, blinking at me like I'm a ghost. "Holy shit. You're back."

She leaps off the bed in a tangle of limbs, racing across the room to throw her arms around my shoulders. I close my eyes, gritting my teeth as I hug her back. Her arms are too thin. I can feel her bones poking through her papery skin, grating against my bones.

I know the feeling is exaggerated—leftover jitteriness from all the drugs I was on—but I squirm away from her anyway.

She frowns. "I was seriously freaked out. They wouldn't tell me where they'd taken you."

I sink onto my bed, pulling my knees to my chest. "Solitary."

"Shit." Sofia's face falls. She lowers herself to the bed opposite me. "You don't look great."

"Think I can request a facial?" It's supposed to be a joke, but my voice falls flat. Harper, Mara, and I used to text each other when we found deals for fifty-dollar facials at this cute place around the corner from Harper's house. Now the idea of that much decadence seems ludicrous.

The corner of Sofia's lip twitches. "Seriously," she asks, "you okay?"

I wrap my arms around myself, pressing my fingers into my shoulder blades. I haven't given much thought to whether I'm okay. The last few days have felt like a bad dream, one I've spent all my energy trying to wake up from. The life I used to have—the one with facials and pancakes with whipped cream faces and nail polish art—seems like it belongs to someone else.

Now that I know I'm awake, I just feel . . . numb.

Sofia scoots to the edge of her bed when I don't answer her question. "What they did to you sucked. You were all set to go home, and they just decided to keep you here? That's messed up."

I swallow. After a moment I say, "That's not exactly what happened."

Another frown. "What do you mean?"

I roll my lip between my teeth. Part of me still doesn't want to admit it out loud. But that's always been my problem, hasn't it? I won't admit my sins. I'd rather make up some happy story than tell the truth.

"I lied. In therapy," I say finally. "Dr. Andrews found out."

Sofia blows air out through her teeth. "Shit," she says again.

"I didn't think it was a big deal . . ." I trail off, considering this, and then try again. "No, that's not true. I knew it was a big deal. I just didn't think she'd find out."

Sofia doesn't say *I told you so*, even though she has every right. She picks up her book and taps a finger against the spine. "What are you going to do now?"

"I don't know." I close my eyes and press my fingers into the lids, rubbing in slow circles. I think of that cold, empty room, the restraints digging into my wrists, and I hold back a shudder. "I never want to go back there." I open my eyes, blinking. "How did you survive a *month*?"

Sofia stares back at me, her face oddly vacant. "It was rough."

"It was *torture*."

"It's not too late. Just tell Dr. Andrews what she wants to hear. Get the fuck out of here."

I stare at Sofia's twitching finger. *Tap tap tap.* Like she's releasing a sudden burst of energy. I shake my head and look away. "You think?"

"When's your next therapy session? Tomorrow?" I nod, and she says, "Do it then. Tell Andrews exactly what happened. She can't keep you here forever."

Exactly what happened. I think of Tayla, lining her eyes in wobbly black lines. Asking me if she can borrow a top for Mara's big end-of-the-year party.

"You don't have to go," I'd told Tayla, annoyed. "I know you don't want to."

Her, answering with a shrug, "They're my friends, too."

But they weren't, really. Not anymore. Harper and Mara were my friends. Tayla just hung out with us.

My mouth feels dry, but I make myself smile. "You make it sound easy."

"The truth is never easy," Sofia says. She leans back against the wall, feet dangling over the edge of her bed. "If it were, I'd be long gone by now."

"You'll get there," I say, and my voice cracks. "Both of us will. We're getting out of here and never looking back, I fucking swear it."

Sofia scratches her tattoo. The scab had just started to heal, but the corner of her nail flicks against it, drawing blood. A drop falls onto her bed, blossoming on the white sheets like a flower.

She presses her thumb into the fabric, soaking it up. "I know we will," she says.

# CHAPTER 18

## *After*

Elyse removes my leather jacket, ripping lining and breaking zippers, her fingernails snaring on skin. I try to fight—hands clawing, elbows swinging—but I feel clumsy and uncoordinated, my body moving much too slowly. She jabs her shoulder into my collarbone, easily pinning me against the wall.

Her face is close to mine, teeth bared like she's about to bite. "How do you like us now, college girl?"

She spits the last two words. *College girl.* My brain is still sludgy with booze and drugs. I blink and say, through clenched teeth, "You're doing this because you're jealous of some *students?*"

A slow shake of her head. "You American girls are all alike. You are like vermin in this town. Like rats crawling in where nobody wants you, patting yourselves on the back because tourism brings us poor Italians money." Her upper lip curls. "You never think of what you take away just by being here."

I remember the expression on Francesca's face while she served wine at Professor Coletti's. That vague, blank stare.

*They think they understand us because they know one of our stories.*

In the story, Lucia's sacrifice drives out all the other sinners. Do they really think that sacrificing *me* will drive out the American students?

"Look, if you let me go, I'll get my friends to leave, okay?" My brain is working as fast as it can, trying to think of something, anything, I can offer her. "We'll be out of your town tonight, I *swear*."

"Just three girls? What difference will that make?"

She's right, it's not a logical solution, but I can't seem to get my brain working properly. Everything seems muddy and confusing. I throw my weight against Elyse's hands, trying to push her off me. "I'm not even a student, you *freak*!"

"Stupid girl. We didn't take you because you are a student. We took you because you are *diavolina*."

"*Think*," Angelica says, interrupting her own chant. "We *think* she is *diavolina*. We agreed to test her first."

The word *test* zips down my spine like a warning. Elyse turns, shifting her weight off my collarbone. She says something in Italian, but I barely hear her. Something black flashes in the corner, just beyond her shoulder. It's so dark down here I thought it was just a patch of shadow. But it's not.

It's a doorway. A second door, leading to God knows where. I glance at the exit we came down, but Francesca has planted herself in front of it, blocking the way out. This second doorway might be my only chance of escape.

I swallow, trying to gather energy in my muscles. I still feel slow, sluggish, weighted down with drugs and booze and fear, but I think of stories I've heard of mothers who get crazy spurts of adrenaline when their children are in danger, how they manage to lift cars and run crazy distances.

"You made a *promise*, Francesca," Angelica says. She hugs the Bible closer to her chest. "We said—"

I push myself off the wall, lunging for the doorway. I catch the flip of Elyse's hair as she spins around and hear Francesca shout something that sounds like a curse. Blood fills my ears, and my vision narrows to a pinpoint. The doorway is so close.

I wrap my fingers around the corner of the wall and

use the momentum to propel myself into the dark. I have one foot down the tunnel—

Fingers tangle in my hair, and I'm jerked back, gasping. Elyse's knuckles come down hard across my cheekbone. I stumble, knocking over a candle as I fall to the ground. Pain lights up the side of my face.

Elyse kneels in front of me. She takes my chin in one hand, squeezing my cheeks until my lips purse. "Do not make this harder than it has to be."

I want to spit at her. But my tongue is too dry, the side of my face huge and pulsing. I can still see the edge of the door out of the corner of my eye, my last chance of escape. I can't seem to catch my breath.

"That'll do," Francesca says, sounding bored. Elyse wrinkles her nose, giving my cheeks one final squeeze. She lets go, and I lurch forward, gasping.

*I'm going to die down here*, I think. And then I squeeze my eyes shut, pushing that thought away. It isn't helpful. I need to *think*. I need to come up with a plan.

But even I can see that the idea is ludicrous. *Plan?* I'm deep underground with three crazy girls, outnumbered, and coming down hard from a night of partying. A plan isn't going to get me out of this. I'll need a miracle.

"We are wasting time." Francesca tilts her head, eyes traveling over the black lace and nude silk of my teddy. "Let's begin."

*Begin.* The word sends something vicious twisting through me. Angelica's voice wavers as she restarts her chant. *"Jú . . . júdica Dómine nocéntes . . . me; expúgna impugnántes me . . ."*

Elyse grabs a handful of my hair and yanks me upright. Pain flares through my scalp.

"Get off!" I struggle to steady my breathing. "Begin what? What are you going to do to me?"

She tugs my hands behind my back, snickering under her breath.

*This isn't happening,* I think. *It's a joke. It's a dream. It's . . .*

But when I open my eyes again, Francesca is in front of me. Candlelight flickers behind her, leaving her face in darkness. I don't see her lips move as she says, "Are you ready?"

My head spins wildly, trying to make sense of what's about to happen. *Test.* They said something about a test. That means there's a way to pass and a way to fail. If I pass, I can't be a *diavolina,* right? Elyse and Francesca want to hurt me, but Angelica is here only because she really thinks I'm evil. If I pass the test, she'll make them let me go.

Hope blooms inside my chest. I still have a chance of getting out of here.

Elyse pinches the back of my neck and shoves me into

the middle of the room. I stumble, grabbing the table to keep from falling.

"Up you go," Elyse says.

I curl my fingers around the edge of the table. It feels rickety, the wood at least a hundred years old and covered in layers of dust and grime.

And something else. Something that looks a lot like blood. I swallow and look away. "You want me to climb onto this thing?"

"I won't ask twice."

My eyes dart left and right, but there are no other options, no way out. Heat seems to press in around me, making the air tremble.

Arms shaking, I pull myself onto the table. It's massive, several feet longer than my body. The wooden legs groan when I lower myself to my back, but they hold.

There are wooden levers attached to either end of the wood, each holding a coil of rope. My eyes flick over the ropes and then away again. I don't want to look at them directly. Don't want to think too hard about what they're for.

*This is a test*, I think, clenching and unclenching my hands. If I pass, maybe everything will be okay.

For a moment, the only sound in the small room is Angelica's voice. *"Confundántur et revereántur quaeréntes ánimam meam . . ."*

Francesca removes a small knife from her pocket and flicks it open. The blade catches the candlelight, glinting silver and gold. My heart leaps into my chest. I curl my fingers into the wood.

"In the old days, villagers would talk of a devil's mark, a spot on a *diavolina*'s body that does not feel any pain. You can stab and stab this piece of flesh, and still the whore will not bleed. Let's see if we can find your mark."

I can't take my eyes off the knife blade. Francesca tilts it back and forth, just before my face, causing the flickering gold light to move up and down its edge.

I think of leaping off the table now, pushing past Francesca, running desperately for the doorway again. But Elyse stands just behind her, arms crossed over her chest, looking like she'd love another reason to hit me.

I shift my eyes to the low ceiling, trying hard to keep my breathing steady.

*This is a test . . .*

Francesca leans forward, resting the blade against my cheek without actually cutting me. The cold metal feels like a salve on my hot skin. "This is how we will know if you are *diavolina*. We will cut you and see if you bleed."

A shaky breath rattles my lungs. The hair on my arms stands straight up.

*It's a test*, I tell myself. *I just have to find a way to pass.*

Francesca removes the knife from my cheek, and a cold wave of relief washes over me. I don't dare move or breathe, convinced that any sudden movement will cause her to press the blade to my skin again. Francesca stares down at me, a strangely detached expression on her face, like she's thinking something through. Then she begins to unwind the thick rope from the levers at the ends of the table.

I start to jerk my arm back, but Elyse shifts forward, eyebrow cocked, a hungry look flashing through her eyes. I force myself to stay still as Francesca wraps the rope around my wrists. Pulls tight.

Francesca moves to my feet, winding the same coarse rope around my ankles so that I'm tied to the table. She hums while she works, a single clear note that interrupts Angelica's even chanting.

*"Avertántur retrórsum et confundántur, cogitántes míhi mála . . ."*

I lie very still, afraid that any movement might send the table—and *me*—crashing to the ground. Francesca gives the ropes at my ankles one final pull to make sure they're tight enough. And then she reaches for the lever.

There's a groan of wood, a creak of rope. Sharp fibers dig into my skin. The bindings at my ankles grow taut.

"What's going on?" My voice sounds high and fluttery. "What're you doing?"

Francesca's humming doesn't falter. She moves to the lever near my hands.

I know what's going to happen. The ropes will pull

on my ankles and wrists; my body will stretch. I even move my arms over my head so the pain won't be so bad, telling myself that it'll all be over soon. I squeeze my eyes shut when I hear the wood moan. I hold my breath.

Nothing prepares me for what comes next.

My arms and legs jerk into line, muscles taut as rubber bands. My spine lifts off the table. I want to cry or scream, but the pressure steals my voice and the only thing I can manage is a sharp gasp, my lips quivering. I suddenly feel foolish for lying so still as she tied me to this table, for doing nothing to get away. But what was there to do? Even now this room feels claustrophobic and boiling, my brain too sluggish to find a way out.

Finally, Francesca moves away from the lever. I feel a brief flare of relief. One more crank and my body would just rip apart, like a rag doll, nothing more than cotton and fabric and loose stitches.

*Then—*

The pocketknife swipes down my cheek with a flick of Francesca's wrist, pain like fire lighting through my skin. A sudden slash on my opposite cheek comes next, the movement just as quick. A spasm moves through me like a wave. My body convulses, trying to fold in on itself, but the bindings at my wrists and ankles tighten, holding me in place. I hear a low *pop* followed by pain flaring in my shoulder.

"There is so much skin to test." Francesca holds the bloody knife up to my face. "We will be here all night."

I want to curl into a ball. But I can't cringe or flinch, can't cover myself with my hands; the ropes are too tight. There's nothing I can do to protect my body. I release a ragged, defeated sob. My voice doesn't sound human.

But it doesn't matter; I can see now that my plan was flawed. There's too much skin.

I pull with my arm, testing the ropes at my wrist to see if there's still a way to wriggle free. But they're too tight. My fingers are starting to go numb as the circulation in my arm gets cut off.

Slowly, Francesca drags the knife across my belly. I hear the rip of fabric and lace and steel myself, eyes clenched shut, waiting for the pain.

It doesn't hit right away. I struggle to look down, and I catch a flash of red. My chest heaves with panic, blocking the blood from view. It takes a second for my nerves to flare as they register that my skin is being split apart.

My brain screams: *This is a test, this is a test, this is a test . . .*

I can't make myself scream anymore. My mouth falls open, but all my energy has gone to dealing with the pain, trying to keep myself from passing out.

*They'll get tired of this.* I hope—I pray—they'll get bored. *They'll stop, they have to stop.*

She slashes again.

Again.

They're shallow cuts, deep enough to break the skin without doing any real damage. But the pain is like fire. Blood runs down my arms and legs and gathers on the table beneath me. As much as the cuts hurt, it's the blood that bothers me more than anything. It's sticky and warm, reminding me that it was inside my body just seconds ago.

And now it's pooling on the dirty wood. Forming a little stream that drips over the side and onto the floor, staining the dirt red.

Francesca takes a step back, wiping her knife on her white dress. She studies me, one eyebrow flicked.

"Please . . . stop." My face crumples. I feel the muscles around my eyes and mouth spasm, unable to hold my expression together through the pain. A desperate, involuntary groan escapes my lips. "*Please.* I'm not a devil. I didn't do anything wrong."

Francesca blinks, impassive. It's like I'm not human. Like the pain I'm experiencing is a trick I'm playing on her.

I swallow my fear and tilt my head up, meeting Francesca's eyes. "You didn't find the mark, did you? You know I'm telling the truth."

Francesca holds the knife out to Elyse. "We didn't find it yet. But we will."

"My turn," Elyse says. Something twisted flashes through her eyes. Yearning. Desire. "I will enjoy this, *diavolina*."

The blade rips the skin on my shoulder. It cuts into the patch of bare skin above the line of my underwear. It slashes into my belly button.

The room around me seems to grow darker until I can't see anything but heavy shadows. The floor tilts and sways. The fear I'd been trying not to feel hits now.

There's no way for me to pass this test. They'll just cut and cut until there's no more skin left. Until all the blood has drained from my body. Until I'm dead.

# CHAPTER 19

The knife bites into my ribs. It's just a nick, but I feel my skin separating around the blade, the hot gush of blood bubbling up to meet the wound. I open my mouth in a wordless scream. The sound that comes out of me is more animal than human.

My scream fades, and Angelica's chant rushes in to fill the silence. *"Fíant táamquam púlvis ante fáciem vénti: et Ángelus Dómini coárctans eos . . ."*

*Then—*

Cold metal moves up the side of my stomach. "I have been working in the butcher shop with my father since I was a little girl." Elyse catches my eye, the corner of her mouth curling as she drags the knife over my body. She presses just hard enough to drive the edge of the blade into my skin without actually cutting it open. "One of the things he taught me was how to take a pig apart piece by piece, using only a knife."

I crane my neck, lifting my head to watch the line of red appear, raw and throbbing.

She's trying to psych me out. I won't let her. If there's no way to pass this test, then my only hope is to stay conscious. Reserve my strength. Wait for them to make a mistake.

I remember a PE class years ago, the teacher barking at us to do push-ups.

"Your brain will fail a thousand times before your body will," she said as we struggled to pump our arms. I think of that now as my body burns and shivers. I tell myself, *If I can keep my brain calm, my body will be okay.* Right now, that seems like an impossible task.

But I swallow and say, as calmly as I can manage, "Why are you telling me this?"

I catch the edge of Elyse's massive shoulder from the corner of my eye. It jerks up and down in a shrug. "I always wondered whether this would work on a person, too. Whether I could take someone apart piece by piece. Like they were meat. I guess we shall see."

My breath comes in short bursts. My mind spins

inside my head, throwing up image after image. That small knife separating my skin like tissue paper, sliding into the joints between my shoulder and arm with a *pop*. I picture Elyse angling the blade away from her, and I hear the sick, wet sound of muscle and skin tearing as she carves my arm away from my body . . .

My chest heaves. I can't quite inhale.

"Please," I force out. "You won't find anything. I'm not—"

Elyse shuts me up with a swift jab to my shoulder. The blade sinks too deep, too fast, and air rushes out of my lungs, like a punctured balloon. The room around me swims in and out of focus.

*This is it*, I think. My shoulders tense up. I hold my breath . . .

Francesca raises her hand. *"Abbastanza."*

I don't recognize the word, but Elyse moves away from me. Blood runs down my arms and legs in ribbons. I can't stop shaking. It feels like there isn't an inch of skin on my body that hasn't been poked or sliced.

*They've failed*, I think, desperately. *They didn't find anything. They couldn't have found anything* . . .

But I know it doesn't matter. They won't let me out of here. If I want out, I have to get myself out.

I blink, my eyelids sticking together for a moment before I manage to force them open again. I can no longer tell the girls apart. Elyse's dark, hateful eyes merge with Angelica's twitchy ones. I can't tell if the sneering lips floating above me are Francesca's or not.

It's a while before I realize that Angelica has stopped chanting. When I manage to separate their faces, hers is the one that comes into clearest focus. She's angled toward the door, head tilted. Something catches and flares in her eye: fear.

She says something urgent in Italian and jerks her head toward the tunnel.

The silence in the small room pulses as the rest of us go quiet, straining to hear what Angelica hears. After a moment, I catch it:

Creaking. Slow and steady, like footsteps. A slice of a laugh. Low, echoing voices.

"Help me!" My voice bursts from my mouth like a desperate thing, shrill and cracking. *This is it.* My one chance at escape. I thrash against the ropes holding me to the table, no longer caring how badly they pull at my wrists. "Please! Help me! Help—"

Elyse's hand comes down fast, whipping my head to the side. My ear slams into the wooden table, sending it rocking. Pain pulses through my bones.

"Shut up," Elyse snaps, cracking her knuckles. But her voice is quiet, and her gaze slides off me, moving back to the tunnel.

The voices have gone quiet. The footsteps are slower. They heard me.

I stretch out my jaw, but I don't dare scream again. Elyse has tightened her grip on the knife, and she's got her body angled toward me, as though she'd like nothing better than to sink the blade into my chest. I glance, desperately, at Francesca. She's the leader, after all. She'll tell Elyse to back off. To wait. But Francesca doesn't do anything.

Angelica says something in Italian, and Francesca spits back an answer. Her eyes are massive, her teeth working hard at her lower lip.

She says, "They can't find her here."

"So go talk to them, make some excuse," Elyse says. Her fingers curl around the handle of the knife, possessive.

Angelica's eyebrows go up. "Alone?" she says, voice high with nerves. "But why would Francesca be here alone on festival night? They will know she's hiding something."

More creaking from above. A hushed voice.

"You'll come with me." Francesca jerks her chin at Elyse. "We will make something up."

Elyse glances from me to the knife. "But—"

Francesca releases a sharp reprimand in Italian, and Elyse closes her mouth. Nods.

"Angelica, you stay here." Francesca looks down at

me and licks her lips. "But wait outside the door. It is bad luck to be alone with the devil. She lies."

Angelica straightens. "I know not to listen to the devil's lies."

Francesca leans over me. She's trying to keep her expression calm, like everything's under control, but I can see the fear streaked across her face. She anxiously tucks a strand of green hair behind her ear. To Angelica, she says, "If you are sure. But be careful. Don't listen to anything she says."

I want to laugh, but the pain prickling over my skin keeps me silent. I roll my lower lip between my teeth to keep my mouth from twitching. This is it. They're losing control. It's my chance to get out.

"We will be back," Francesca says to me. "If you say anything, if you scream again, we will kill you."

*You're going to kill me anyway*, I think as she storms from the room, Elyse trailing at her heels. Angelica flinches and darts out of their way. I hear the pad of their shoes hurrying up the tunnel's dirt floor.

I turn my head to the side, studying Angelica. The candlelight turns her skin gold. Her dark curls look angelic beneath the thin film of white lace.

She's different from the other two. Crazy and pious, but not violent like Elyse. I think of how sweet she was when I first met her at the church. How she offered me her chair and acted concerned when I burned my wrist on candle wax. If any one of them might let me go, it's her.

"Angelica," I whisper.

She flinches, dark eyes darting over to me. "You are supposed to stay quiet."

"You know I'm not a *diavolina*, Angelica."

She taps her fingers against the spine of her Bible, her movements fast and jerky.

"They never found a mark," I plead. "I'm innocent."

She licks her lips, eyes moving up, toward the ceiling. Someone upstairs has started playing music. The sound seeps through the dirt, trembling in the air around us.

My chest constricts. Now it doesn't matter if I scream; they'll never hear me over the music. I swallow, my eyes darting toward the door. I'm running out of time.

I say again, urgently, "I'm *innocent*. What you're doing is wrong."

Angelica hisses, "*Diavolina lies*." The cruel twist of her voice raises the hair on the back of my neck. "Francesca was right. It is dangerous to be alone with you."

She presses her hands to her ears and hurries into the tunnel to wait by the door, where my demonic lies cannot reach her.

This is it. For a moment, I can't breathe. Then the air in the small room sharpens to a knifepoint. This is my chance to escape. I glance at the other door, the one that leads deeper into Cambria's underground tunnels. I have maybe five minutes before one of them comes back. Maybe less.

The ropes around my wrists feel tighter all of a sudden. I give a gentle tug—testing—and pain like fire shoots down my arm. My shoulders ache. I dig my teeth into my lower lip, focusing on that sharp pain so that I don't obsess over the deep, dull throb in my arms. I *twist*. Sharp fibers dig into my skin, and something burns through my bones.

The candlewicks seem to spark and grow, flames stretching up the sides of the wall. Their shadows look like wild, reckless things. I pull harder. Twist and squirm. It might be my imagination, but the ropes holding me to the table seem to loosen. I release a shallow, desperate gasp. *Come on.*

A voice booms through the tunnel, sending the hair on my neck straight up. It came from above. Laughter? Screaming? I can't tell. It bounces off the packed-dirt walls, turning into something unrecognizable. I'm running out of time. Any second, all three of them will be back down here with me, tightening my restraints, laughing at my futile attempt at escape.

I yank my arm down, pulling until tears spring to my eyes. A taste like copper fills my mouth, and blood gathers on my tongue, thick and hot. I bit straight through my lip.

I pull harder.

Something's happening above me. I hear the heavy thud of footsteps. A laugh. Voices rising and falling.

And then, closer—

*Squeaking.* Like rusty hinges.

I go still, listening. I feel a shift in the energy of the room. A prickle in the air. There's something down here with me.

The squeaking comes closer. I twist my head to the side, my heartbeat pounding in my ears. The shadows on the wall twitch with movement. My skin starts to crawl as I realize what it must be. The sweat on my chest goes cold.

"No!" I say in a hard whisper. I rock back and forth, shaking the table to try to scare it. "Go away!"

I know the second it climbs onto the table's legs, its claws sending tiny vibrations shuddering through the wood. I want to shout for help, to beg Angelica to come back and scare it away. The only thing that stops me is the knowledge that I'd be giving up my one chance of escape. I hold my breath, craning my neck.

The rat crawls onto the table between my feet. Its fur is albino white, like it's never seen the sun, red eyes glistening like drops of blood. My breath catches in my chest, and my heart goes hard and slow, like drumbeats. The rat rises to its hind legs and lifts its face, nose twitching. That's when I realize:

It *smells* me. This thing has come for my blood.

"Go!" I hiss. I yank at my restraints. My movements are jerky and desperate now. I no longer care about ripping skin or yanking my shoulder out of its joint. I just want *out*.

The rat falls back on all fours with a shudder that vibrates through the table. It's *huge*, the size of a small cat. I try to kick it away, but the ropes around my ankles hold tight, and my feet just flop back and forth, useless. My neck aches from the strain of holding up my head.

The rat crawls up to my calf. Sniffs.

"No!" I try to kick, but all I manage is a twitch of my big toe.

The rat sinks its yellow teeth deep into my flesh.

It's different from the knife. Then, the pain was immediate, white-hot and burning. The hurt flared for a brief, terrible instant before fading to a throb.

This is worse. I hear the wet smack of teeth long before the first dizzy wave of pain washes over me. This pain isn't clean; it's *gnawing*. I release a strangled cry and let my head drop back to the table, the fight seeping out of me. My stomach clenches. Nausea climbs up my throat. My body jerks—trying to fold in on itself—but the ropes hold me tight.

*I need to get out*, I think, desperate. *I need to escape. They're coming . . .*

But I can't make myself move. For long, grainy

stretches I fall in and out of consciousness, the wet slap of the rat's tongue echoing through my head. Then, just when I think the darkness will pull me under, the monster's teeth sink into new flesh, jolting me awake with a fresh flare of nerves.

This is what it feels like to be eaten alive.

I don't hear the sound of footsteps, don't realize someone's in the room with me until I see Angelica leaning over me, shooing the rat away. The table shifts as the creature leaps to the floor and skitters back into the tunnel.

And then: a cool hand on my cheek. I struggle to open my eyes through the pain.

Angelica pauses to find the right words. "Are you okay?"

*"Please."* My cheeks feel damp—I'm crying again. I lock eyes with Angelica, trying to find the humanity within those deep pools of black. "Please, I promise you I'm telling the truth. I'm innocent. You have to let me go. *Please.*"

Angelica tilts her head, studying me. *She's not a sadist like Elyse,* I tell myself, praying it's true. She's not blinded by jealousy, like Francesca. She knows that what they're doing is wrong.

Slowly, Angelica moves toward my wrists. A moment later I feel fingers working through the ropes around my hand.

*"Grazie,"* I sputter, gasping. The tears come hot and fast

now, relief cooling my pain like a salve. My chest heaves with sobs. "*Grazie.* Thank you. Oh God, thank you."

The rope falls away, but Angelica doesn't let go of my hand. I feel her fingers pressing into my palm. She twists around, holding my arm up to my face like she wants to show me something. I blink, confused.

"Shh," she murmurs. She takes a candle from the floor and tilts it over my wrist, sending a single drop of wax onto my skin.

"Shit!" I try to pull away, bracing for the pain, but it doesn't come. After all that torture, the wax feels soothing. Like a salve. After a moment, Angelica brushes the drop of white wax off my wrist, angles my arm toward me. The skin below is pale and perfect. Not the slightest hint of red.

"You see?" she says, gesturing. "No burn."

My voice feels thick. "So? What does that mean?"

"It means we have found your devil's mark," Francesca says from the doorway. "Now we know that you are *diavolina.*"

# CHAPTER 20

The room around me shifts in and out of focus, the air shivering like heat coming off a sidewalk. Dazed, I drift from consciousness to sleep and back again. The crosses hanging from the walls seem to peer down at me. How did I end up here—trapped and confined just when I was finally free? Maybe Francesca and her friends were right. I guess it's easier to believe that—to believe I *deserve* this—than it is to believe that terrible things sometimes happen for no reason at all.

The crosses flicker in the candlelight as I struggle to keep my eyes open.

Angelica and Elyse work their fingers through the

bindings at my ankles and wrists. Angelica's movements are careful—almost gentle—but Elyse seems to relish digging her nails into the wounds the ropes left in my skin. I attempt to lift a hand and swat her away, but I can't manage to raise it more than an inch or two before exhaustion floods up my arm, leaving my muscles heavy. Shadows zip across my eyesight, but I can't tell if they're real—something moving in the corners—or a product of my imagination.

Francesca slips her hands under my armpits and pulls me to my feet. Elyse and Angelica move in behind us, each taking an arm to hold me steady. Everything feels slow and clumsy and impossible. Francesca says something, but I can't think past the pain pounding through me. *Fight*, I tell myself. But I can't, not anymore. It's over. I dig my toes into the ground, trying to hold myself steady.

I sway . . .

And then my cheek slams into the packed-dirt floor.

Francesca's face is suddenly inches from mine, candlelight reflected in her hateful eyes.

*"Diavolina."* Her lips curl lovingly around the word. "You have to get up now. We have so much more to do."

"Let me go. *Please*," I beg. Pain rips through my chest, and then I'm choking. The stuff I spit onto the dirt is dark and tacky and tastes like pennies.

*Blood.* I'm spitting up blood.

Francesca's laugh is light and clear. It doesn't sound human.

Angelica reties my ankles and moves on to my wrists. I can tell it's Angelica—her small, nervous fingers give her away. She pulls on my bound arms, groaning, and suddenly I'm on my knees, doubled over. I feel the prick of a knife at my lower back.

"Get up," Francesca says, pushing the blade into my bare skin. There's a part of me that wants to fall backward, lean into it, get this over with.

Instead, I pull my legs beneath my trembling body, standing. My feet seem to move on their own, shuffling slowly along the dirt floor.

A sharp jab from the knife. "Keep moving."

Francesca leads me back through the underground tunnel and into the church courtyard. A few Solo cups still litter the ground, and a devil's mask sits next to the wall, its face creased and torn. Music pours through the streets. I pray for a group of partiers to stumble past. To find me, *help* me. But there's no one.

We walk past the long-dry fountain to a crumbling wall that marks the edge of the city. And then we're pushing through a hole in the brick, standing at the foot of the hill where Lucia was sacrificed. The music sounds louder here. A steady beat pulsing through the street, vibrations tickling the soles of my feet.

*I could run toward the music*, I think. It sounds so close. If I caught them off guard I could slip past, scream for help. I feel a little stronger now that I'm no longer in that stuffy underground room. I could still get away.

As though reading my mind, Elyse digs her fingers deeper into my upper arms, bruising my skin. She pushes into my back, and I stumble forward, pebbles biting into the bottoms of my feet. Angelica hovers at my other shoulder, just out of eyesight. Her shadow stretches before her like a warning.

We make our way through the trees and up the hill, Francesca trailing along behind us. I keep my eyes peeled for a chance to pull away, to run. But the trees are close around us, and I'm barefoot and beaten. I'd never be able to outrun all three of them, I realize.

"Where are we going?" I mumble, defeated. My eyesight starts to swim. I'm going to pass out . . .

Francesca smiles, not kindly. "You will see."

When I come to again, I'm in a packed-dirt clearing at the top of a hill, a tall, wooden stake protruding from the ground in front of me. The stake looks centuries old, the wood splintered and peeling. There's a plaque in front of it, but I can't make out what it says in the dark.

"This is where they brought Lucia," Francesca says, when she sees that I'm awake. She wipes an arm over her forehead to dry the sweat beading along her skin.

"That little whore saved our village many years ago. Now you will do the same."

I swallow, hard. A cold gray lake appears through the branches. Thick white candles have been lined up around the water. Wax drips over their sides and spills onto the rocks below them.

"How?"

"It is okay." Angelica gathers a strand of my hair in her fingers and pushes it behind my ear, gently. "You're lucky that we're doing this for you. This is how you'll become right with God."

"We're going to save you." Sarcasm drips from Elyse's voice, and a smirk curls the corner of her mouth. "It is time for you to be baptized, *diavolina*."

They've crowded in behind me, forcing me to the edge of the lake.

"No." My throat is still scratchy, and the word hurts to say. I throw my weight back, but the girls are laughing now, three sets of hands pressed into my shoulders and moving up my spine, pushing me forward. I tug at the ropes around my wrists, but they don't give. "I don't want to go—"

I stumble and fall, the rest of my voice ripping from my throat. The nerves in my toes flare as my feet hit the icy water. The surface of the lake smacks into my face. I don't have time to catch my breath. Water sloshes over my head, and then I'm sinking.

I don't have time to think about what's happening as I sink to the bottom of the lake. The water above looks green and murky, the surface far away. Dirty water stings my cuts, making them flare with pain. My lungs feel like they're about to burst.

*This is how I die*, I think. I wiggle my shoulders, but my hands are tied behind my back. There's no way to swim, no way to save myself.

The lake is deeper than I thought it would be. I seem to sink forever. I stretch my toes as far as they'll go, thinking I could push myself off from the bottom, but I feel only water. I kick wildly, but without the use of my arms, I can't make myself rise back to the surface. I thrash against the ropes, and that seems to makes me fall faster.

*I don't want to die down here*, I think. I really don't want to die. But my eyesight is already flickering in and out. My lungs burn.

Desperate, I inhale a lungful of lake water, and everything in my head clouds. I start choking. I'm losing oxygen. It won't take long for my lungs to give out, my body to fail. Everything is so dark . . .

I yank at the ropes around my wrists. If I can get my hands free, I might be able to fight my way back to the surface before I fall unconscious.

I pull my wrists apart until tears flood my eyes and the ropes make my fingers go numb. Still, they hold. My skin begins to tear. I feel the warmth of blood gather around my wrists.

I gasp, accidentally inhaling more lake water. My eyesight starts to blur at the edges . . .

And then, with one final, violent tug, I pull an arm free.

For a moment, I seem to have forgotten what I'm supposed to do with it. It feels long and ungainly, half-numb from the rope cutting off my circulation. Then, desperately, I start to claw at the water around me.

My head spins. There's no air left in my lungs, no energy in my muscles. My arms and legs don't feel connected to my body anymore. The water seems to press in on me, holding me down. Every movement is harder than the one before it.

Tiny pinpricks of light hover past the surface of the water. I push. Kick. Claw. The lights grow closer.

*Almost there . . .*

And then, finally, I break through, gasping. The air tastes like it's been coated with sugar. I swim toward the shore and lurch forward, falling to my hands and knees, half crawling, half swimming the rest of the way to land. A shadow falls over me. I lift my head.

"I almost died," I gasp.

"But you didn't die." Francesca grabs a handful of my hair to drag me the rest of the way out of the water. "You were saved."

# CHAPTER 21

Goose bumps cover my arms and legs. Every brush of wind has me shivering and grinding my teeth. My skin has gone numb. I can no longer feel the bite of rocks against my palms or the sticks digging into my shins. I release a deep, hacking cough, spitting up lake water.

"What's the matter?" Francesca purrs, kneeling beside me. "Having trouble breathing?"

"Please," I gasp. Blood leaks from my body in a slow trickle, pooling between my fingers. "Please don't—"

"Breathe through this."

I realize, too late, that she's scooping up a handful of mud. Elyse and Angelica catch me by the arms, holding me steady as Francesca shoves the mud past my clenched lips and into my mouth.

The smell fills my nose and clogs my head. There's cow shit mixed in with the mud, and the rank taste clings to my tongue and the back of my throat. I wrench my head away violently, and Francesca cackles, shoving more of it past my teeth and down my throat.

My stomach clenches. Before I can stop to think about what's going to happen, I double over, vomiting onto the dirt path. The puke tastes terrible, like shit and lake water and blood. A sharp acid taste climbs my throat, but I don't stop. I heave until my entire body is empty. It takes me a long time to catch my breath.

"Let me go." I can still feel mud and shit on my teeth, coating my tongue, clinging to my throat. It's my last, desperate chance at getting away alive. "I'm saved now, right? I repented and I let you baptize me. Now, please, you have to let me go."

Something in Francesca's face changes. The anger in her eyes dims, her lip twitches. For a moment, she reminds me of the girl I met my first night here—the cool bartender who gave me free shots and welcomed me to Cambria.

"Please," I say again.

"Do you really think we just wanted to baptize you, *diavolina*?" Francesca is shaking her head. "Why would

we bring you to this holy place and save your soul for
nothing in return?"

"We aren't saints," Elyse adds. "You owe us."

"Please, you must understand, Lucia saved our village," Angelica adds solemnly. "Every terrible thing she
did before that moment was washed away by her sacrifice. She was a hero. You are a very lucky girl. The
people who live here will remember you forever."

It reminds me of the first time we met, back in the
church. *"You are very lucky; the candle did not burn you."*

My eyes slide off Angelica's face, moving to the stake
at the center of the clearing. For the first time, I notice
the stack of twigs and firewood piled up beside it.

My eyesight doubles, and the world splits into two.
Everything blurs.

Angelica says, "You will be a hero, just like Lucia."

I'm shaking my head, my movements frantic and jerky.
I can't make myself believe what she's saying.

They're going to tie me to that stake. They're going to
watch me burn to death.

I thrash and flail, but it's no use. My muscles are spent.
Even when I connect with Elyse's shoulder or Angelica's
arm, I don't have the strength to put anything substantial
behind the hit. My blows glance off them like a flat stone
skipping over water.

Elyse drags me over to the stake and shoves my back

against the wood. Splinters dig into my skin, tearing at the remaining ragged fabric of my teddy. Angelica twists my hands behind my back and reties my bindings while Francesca watches from a few feet away. Her face looks ghostly in the flickering red-and-orange candlelight.

My voice escapes in a series of sputters. "Francesca, think about this. It's *murder*. You're murdering an innocent—"

She snorts. "Innocent? You are *diavolina*. The baptism may have washed away your sins, but it doesn't change what you are."

She lights a match. Firelight dances in her black pupils, flickering over her sharp features and twitching mouth. Fear hits my stomach like acid. I suddenly wish I were back in the lake, that I hadn't bothered pulling my wrists free and kicking back to the surface. Drowning seems almost merciful compared to death by fire. I picture the smoke and the flames and . . . a sob chokes up my throat. This is going to *hurt*. Tears start rolling down my cheeks, cool and wet against my hot skin.

I close my eyes a second before Francesca tosses the match at the bundle of sticks near my feet, but I hear the sound of the flame catching. *Whoof.*

My muscles go rubber-band rigid beneath my skin. Smoke seeps past my lips and creeps up my nostrils. It strokes my cheeks, trying to find more ways to crawl into my dying body. It itches the back of my throat and sinks into my lungs. It rubs its gritty face against the cuts hatched along my arms and legs, making them throb.

I hold my breath until I can't take it anymore, and then I release a deep, hacking cough, the ropes holding me upright as I pitch forward. I'm no longer in charge of my limbs; they jerk and twitch all on their own. I feel feral, wild. An animal fighting for its life.

The fire is so *close*. Just inches from my toes. I can practically smell my flesh baking, my hair singeing. After everything I went through at the institute, everything I went through before, it seems so horribly, painfully *wrong* that my life should end here.

A scream rips up my throat as I imagine my skin going black and flaky, fire eating away at my body . . .

There's a noise just beneath the crackling flames. Shouting, I think. Or laughing.

I blink wildly, tears pouring down my cheeks. I wish, more than I've ever wished for anything in my life, that I were at home right now. That I could wake up in my own bed, my mom waiting at the door, ready to fuss over me like she always used to when I had a nightmare. I wish I'd never met Harper and Mara, never come to Italy. The want is so deep, so strong that it steals what's left of my breath.

The smoke has turned the air hazy, blurring the figures on the other side of the fire. They look like mirages.

I squint, trying to make out their faces, but my brain

can't make sense of what it's seeing. First there are two figures. Then four. They merge together like shadows.

The fire is loud in my ears, spitting and crackling. A log shifts, sending a shower of red sparks exploding before me. This is it. The stake won't hold me up for much longer. The fire keeps creeping closer . . .

And then—

"Bella!"

*Giovanni.* A flare of hope catches and dies in my chest. Giovanni can't be here. The smoke is making me hallucinate. A sob bubbles up my throat. I must be close to the end.

"Bella, I am coming!"

I blink, and for a moment I think I can see the pentagrams painted across his bare chest. They glow by the light of the fire, beads of sweat rolling over them. Then the flames press in closer, and the image breaks apart.

The hazy figures are moving now. Spinning wildly, hands clasped together. They're dancing. This, at least, is a small mercy: to spend my last moments thinking of Giovanni, believing he came to save me. I almost smile as I watch them, the heat burning the moisture from my eyes. I blink and blink, but I can't make them focus.

Something tickles the bottoms of my feet. I don't dare look down, even as the warmth grows, becoming

DANIELLE VEGA

white-hot needles pricking at my toes, tongues of fire licking my arches. I imagine my skin bubbling. Turning black. And then the pain flares out, like a candle dying, and I realize the fire has fried my nerves. My feet are burning, but I can't feel them.

I curl my hands into fists behind my back, focusing on the edges of my fingernails digging into my palms. Tiny moon-shaped flares of pain. The feeling grounds me, reminding me that I'm still alive. For a little while, at least.

I hear muffled grunts. Thuds. A shadowy figure jerks away from the dance, arms flailing. I see a flash of silver—a knife.

I squint into the flames, understanding washing over me.

They're not dancing.

They're *fighting*.

"Giovanni?" My voice is hesitant. The hope has flickered to life inside of me once more, but I can barely let myself trust it. Smoke crawls down my throat, making me cough. "Giovanni?"

"I am coming, bella—"

I hear a grunt and, through the haze, watch a figure slam into the dirt. Three other blurry shapes gather around him, reminding me of animals circling prey. The fire makes them look huge, their shadows stretching into the sky, their eyes monstrous. I see a flash of teeth, the glint of a knife. A leg swings forward, slamming into his gut.

"Giovanni!" I shout again. But it's no use. They won't let him near me.

They'll kill him first.

# CHAPTER 22

"Giovanni!" My voice goes hoarse as smoke rushes into my mouth, coating my tongue and throat. Choking, I try again, "*Gio—*"

My cry subsides into a fit of hacking coughs. Francesca and the others have surrounded Giovanni. I can just make out the shadowy circle of their bodies, kicking something curled on the ground. I hear the sound of their feet thumping into his body, his low, desperate grunts.

*I have to help him.* I curl my toes into the twigs and use the leverage to press my back into the stake, trying to create as much distance between the fire and my skin as possible. It shoots higher, red flames dancing wildly against the night sky.

Giovanni reaches for Francesca, trying to pull himself to his feet. She stomps down, and I think I hear something crack.

"Giovanni!"

I lunge forward without thinking, so desperate to get to Giovanni that I momentarily forget about the ropes binding my wrists and the fire crackling beneath me. A spark of red jumps from the woodpile to my knee, and I feel a sudden, sharp singe of heat. I scream, but the flame dies the second it comes into contact with my skin. Then an ember pops, leaping to the spare bit of lace near my shoulder. A curl of orange licks the ropes binding my arms.

I feel the sizzle of heat, followed by a sudden *hiss* that tells me the flames have died.

*I'm still wet from the lake*, I realize. I can feel the flames pressing against my skin, but they can't light, not like they would if I were dry.

I blink a few times, trying to gather my wits despite the black wall of smoke surrounding me. My wet skin might win me a few more minutes, but I already feel the moisture being burned off me as the fire creeps closer. I don't have much longer. If I'm going to get to Giovanni, I need to act fast.

I wriggle in place, testing my restraints. The only spot on my body where the flames feel dangerously hot is around my wrists.

I twist around. A red spark flickers from the ropes binding my hands together. That flame didn't go out. The ropes are the only things besides the twigs that are still dry.

I turn back around, swallowing. The smoke is thick, and it instantly makes me feel dizzy and stupid. I focus on the sound of my heart thudding in my ears, willing my brain to work.

*If the fire eats through the ropes at my wrists, I might be able to pull myself free.* It's a long shot, but it's my only hope at escape.

I lean forward as far as I can go, releasing all my weight so that the burning ropes are the only things holding me upright. I'm close to the flames now. I feel their heat on my nose and cheeks, instantly drying the last of the lake water and turning the mud on my face into a hard, crusty clay. I flex my fingers, testing the ropes at my wrists. They still hold tight.

"Come on," I mutter. I lunge, and a shudder moves down my arms and vibrates through the burning ropes. I cringe, feeling the heat eat into the skin at my wrists. My hands are behind my back, so I can't see what's happening, but I feel my skin tearing, the burning ropes rubbing them raw. Tears spring to my eyes.

*It's a game*, I tell myself. Like when you're little and the mean older kids give you a rope burn by holding your wrists with two hands and twisting the skin in opposite directions. Just a game.

I'm almost able to believe that. The burns at my wrists sort of feel like a rope burn, only a million times worse. I twist my arms apart, tugging, pulling, until—

The ropes give, and I fly forward, stumbling face-first into the growing fire.

My skin isn't damp anymore. I can feel the fire finding my flesh, eating into it hungrily. A scream rips from my throat. I let it loose, howling into the night as I tear through the burning twigs and branches and collapse onto the ground in front of one of the girls—Angelica. I roll around like a dog, twitching and screaming as the dirt begins to suffocate the flames crawling over my body.

Dimly, I'm aware that Angelica is backing away.

"*Diavolina*," she whispers, crossing herself.

*Good*, I think, trembling as I push myself to my feet. I probably look just like the devil right now, with the crusty layer of mud covering my face and flames erupting from my arms and legs. A smile splits my lips—not a real one, but a deranged, desperate smile that cracks the mask of mud on my skin. My fingers curl into claws.

*Let her think I'm evil.* I hope she never forgets the way I look right now. I hope my muddy face and burning body follow her into her dreams.

Giovanni, Elyse, and Francesca are a few feet away, still fighting. Giovanni's on his knees, trying to stand, while Francesca hangs from his shoulders. She's howling, digging into his face with her fingernails, doing everything she can to keep him down. Elyse stands in front of them both, knife clenched in one hand. She's close enough to stab him, but she hesitates, eyes shifting up to Francesca.

Giovanni's strong, but he can't take both of them on at once. I lurch forward, arms outstretched. The darkness beyond pulses, promising escape—but I can't leave Giovanni behind.

I manage a single step toward them before a body slams into me at full force, pushing me into the dirt so hard that the air leaves my chest in a *whoosh*. My forehead snaps into the ground, coming into contact with something hard and sharp. I feel blood well up beneath my skin.

"You cannot walk away from this." Angelica's normally timid voice has lowered to a growl. She digs her fingernails into my skin, squeezing so hard that fresh tears gather in the corners of my eyes. She rolls me onto my back, pressing down on my shoulders with both hands. "You must burn. Our village needs you."

She spits as she talks. A fleck of it lands on my cheek. I grit my teeth, hating her. I don't know if it's the fire or the fact that I came so close to death, but I no longer feel weak and ready to give up. Now I want to fight.

I grab Angelica by the arms and dig my own nails

into her skin. She must not have expected this, because surprise leaps across her face. I throw the entire weight of my body into her, forcing her off me. She slams into the ground with a smack, her head whacking against the packed dirt.

Her face twists. She fumbles for something in her pocket, her movements clumsy. A switchblade.

Using every last ounce of strength in my body, I rip the knife out of her hand and plunge it down. It sinks into something soft and warm. Angelica releases a tiny gasp, her mouth forming a perfect O of surprise. Her chin trembles.

I freeze. Cold oxygen burns through my lungs, making my chest heave. Blood pumps in my ears. I try hard to ignore the feeling of something warm and sticky gathering beneath my fingers.

Then a voice inside my head screams: *What did you do?*
I look down.

The knife is still lodged between Angelica's breasts, the handle slick and red. Blood pumps out of the wound, coming faster than I expect it to, like water from a faucet. Angelica's fingers fumble and clench, trying to hold it in.

"You . . ." Her eyes go wide. Her mouth hangs open for a long moment, struggling to find the words. "You . . . are a sick girl . . ."

*Sick girl.* The words slither through my head. I grab Angelica by the shoulders, shaking her limp body.

"I didn't want this!" My voice sounds shrill—crazy. *Sick girl*, I think, and feel my fingers dig deeper into the sleeves of Angelica's white dress, bruising her skin. My hands are coated with her blood. It seeps into the cracks of my knuckles and pools beneath my fingernails, staining them red. "Why couldn't you just leave me alone?"

Fingers brush against my arm, and I jerk back, heart pounding. It's Giovanni. Three long scratch marks trail down his cheek, glistening with blood.

"Bella," he says, casting a glance over his shoulder. I follow his gaze and see Francesca and Elyse collapsed in a heap on the ground. "We have to go. *Now.*"

For a long moment, I can't make myself move. Elyse's foot twitches. Francesca groans. I don't know what Giovanni did to them, but they won't be down for long.

Angelica lowers a hand to her chest, curling her fingers around the blade still lodged in her body. Her eyes find mine, eyelids flickering.

"Sick girl," she says again. Her eyes go dull.

She's dead. I killed her.

A hand jostles my arm. "Bella!"

I release my fingers one by one. Then, still trembling, I take Giovanni's arm, and the two of us start to run.

# CHAPTER 23

Tree branches scratch my cheeks and snag in my hair. Wind blows past, cooling the sweat on my chest and forehead. Every step I take sends a jerky shudder shooting up my legs. It doesn't slow me down; I run with all my strength. Everything from the trees to the wind to the pain seems strange. Dreamlike. The only thing that feels real is the heat from Giovanni's hand, his fingers curled tightly around my wrist.

The village appears below, golden and glowing in the darkness. Snatches of music blow through the trees, mixing with laughter and voices. The party's still raging. If I squint, I can see the roiling mass of bodies moving in the darkness.

Giovanni's fingers tighten. He skids to a stop just before we reach the wall separating the village from the trees and hills beyond. He pulls me behind him in one easy movement, blocking the path back up the side of the hill with his body. His eyes flicker through the shadows, alert.

"They will follow us," he says, voice rough-edged. "They might be coming now."

"We should call the police. The *polizia* or whatever they're called here."

"Francesca's brother is poliziotto."

A static sound fills my head. *Brother.*

Giovanni nods, as though something in the darkness has satisfied him. He pulls me through the hole in the crumbling stones, one hand pressed against the top of my head so I don't hit it on the wall. "Don't worry. I have an idea."

The narrow streets seem to close in around us as we run. Ancient brick walls rise up, blocking the sounds from the festival. I can't hear the music and voices, but I feel them vibrating through the streets, shuddering up into my toes. Giovanni leads me down an alleyway, turning sharp at a stairwell that seems to appear out of nowhere. And then we're racing down steps, the hard stones cold against my feet.

Halfway down, Giovanni stops, spinning me in place. A spiky wrought-iron fence appears from the shadows.

The catacombs.

My entire body goes stiff. "No," I say, my voice flat.

"Bella, you must listen. We have to get you out of here." Giovanni presses his hands down on my shoulders to hold me steady. The weight of them seems to be the only thing keeping me upright. "This is a small town. An *old* town. The people here will do nothing against one of their own, do you understand?"

"Francesca *tortured* me."

"I know this. But you might be in even more danger now. You must get your friends and get out of here, pronto. These tunnels are the quickest way through our village."

I'm still shaking my head. The darkness beyond the gate seems to pulse. I think of those yellowed skulls lining the walls, their jagged mouths snarling out at me, and shiver involuntarily.

Giovanni reaches through the gate, unlatching something I don't see. I hear the click of metal against metal.

"It is the only way," he says, one hand moving to my back. He pushes me forward, into the dark.

Cold air falls over us. It's silent down here. The kind of silence that seems to be playing a trick on your ears. Even my ragged breathing seems muted by the ancient walls.

We walk slowly. Once we're far enough from the entrance that we no longer see the silvery strips of moonlight, Giovanni pulls out his lighter. The small orange flame does little to chase away the darkness. I crowd close into Giovanni's back, face pressed to his sweaty skin. I can feel my heart beating against his spine.

I look straight ahead, careful not to search the darkness for the skulls, but it's impossible to avoid them completely. I catch a corner of yellowed bone. Hollow, cracked sockets. Broken teeth.

"Only a little farther." Giovanni's voice echoes off the walls, chasing the darkness deeper into the tunnels. "They won't think to look for us here, and these tunnels go all over the village. Once you're back at your apartment, you'll need to pack your things. I can borrow a truck from the store, and we can drive to Florence. You should be safe there until we get you a flight back to America."

I nod, my chin brushing against Giovanni's shoulder. He makes it all sound so simple. "What about my friends? Mara and Harper?"

A beat of silence. Then: "They will have to go with you. After the polizia find out about Angelica, your friends will not be welcome here."

*Angelica.* I think of her blood spurting between my fingers, how her eyes looked up at me, dull and lifeless. My knees tremble so badly they knock together. I sink into Giovanni, no longer able to hold myself up.

He stops walking. "It is all right," he murmurs, pulling me close to him. He kisses the top of my head. "You're okay, right? I'm worried."

I wrap my arms around him, breathing against his chest. Each inhale feels like something ripping apart inside me, something clawing up my throat.

"How did you find me?" I choke out.

"Bella?"

"On the hilltop. I was so sure I was going to die. The fire was so close, and the smoke was making me dizzy. I'd given up, and then you were there." I lift my head, blinking, trying to separate his face from the darkness. "How did you know?"

I feel his hand on my cheek, fingers cool and damp. "I was below, looking for you at the festival, but you were nowhere. Your friends hadn't seen you in hours, and that made me nervous. I started to worry . . ."

He pauses to take a deep, ragged breath. "I've known Francesca a long time, since we were babies. She's always loved the story of Lucia. She used to say that we need to make the same sacrifice today, to make Cambria good again. I always thought she was joking, but . . . Tonight, when I couldn't find you, I got a bad feeling. And then I looked up at the hill and saw the fire . . ."

"I killed her . . ." My voice cracks. "That girl, Angelica."

"She wanted to kill you first."

My chest clenches with my sobs. "But I *stabbed* her. There was so much blood . . ."

Giovanni takes my face in his hands and tilts it up. His breath is warm on my lips. It's too dark down here to see anything, but I can imagine the look on his face. The tender tilt of his eyes, the soft curve of his mouth before he kisses me.

"Berkley," he says in a throaty voice. "You need to listen to me. You did what you had to do. You got away. Everything else . . . that isn't your fault."

His voice comforts me. I find myself nodding, even though he can't see me in the darkness. "Really?"

"You survived, bella. You are alive."

His lips find mine in the darkness. They're warm and salty with sweat. *I'm alive.* I feel the words scream through my body, and I hold him closer. Press my face hard against his.

The kiss grows deeper, hungrier.

*I'm alive*, I think. Heat creeps up my neck. *I'm alive.*

And then—a footstep.

The sound is soft—the barest scrape of a shoe over cobblestones—but it echoes in my ears like a gunshot. I jerk away from Giovanni and spin around, heart hammering as I peer into the darkness. "Did you hear that?"

Giovanni moves in behind me and starts to kiss my neck. "Hear what?"

"It sounded like a footstep."

Giovanni moves away from me. Cold air rushes to fill the space where his body just was. "You are sure?"

"I don't know." It was so close, not more than a few feet from where we're standing. But now my heart is thudding in my ears and I'm staring into the darkness, and there's a part of me that wonders if I heard anything at all. "Maybe I imagined it."

"I should go look, just in case."

"Don't leave me." I can hear the tremor in my voice, but I don't care. I don't want to be down here by myself. "Let's just forget about it, okay? Keep moving?"

"I'll only be gone for a moment." Giovanni's feet shuffle over the packed dirt, fading as he moves farther away. "Stay here. I will be back."

# CHAPTER 24

The dark presses in around me. Giovanni's footsteps fall at even intervals, growing softer as they move farther down the tunnel. I hear the click and flicker of his lighter, and then an orange glow illuminates the black.

Giovanni turns, wiggling his fingers at me. My heart leaps, and for a moment, I forget where we are. I wave back, smiling, ignoring the jagged white teeth leering at us from just beyond Giovanni's circle of light.

He blows me a kiss and then disappears around the corner.

And I'm alone.

At first, I count my heartbeats. I don't have a watch

or a cell phone, so it seems like the easiest way to keep track of how much time passes.

After sixty heartbeats, I'm tapping my foot.

After one hundred and forty, all the hairs on my neck are standing up.

After two hundred, I'm straining to hear anything in the darkness.

Maybe that's why I notice the quick intake of breath. Like someone sighing. Or holding back a laugh.

I press my hand flat against my chest, as though to still the blood pumping through my heart. I hold my breath, listening.

Nothing and more nothing and more nothing. I feel my muscles unclench, my shoulders droop. I drop my hand to my side, relaxing. And then—

A footstep.

I whirl around. My heartbeat—nearly silent a second ago—is now a steady drum pounding in my ears, blocking all other sound. The noise came from behind me.

I creep deeper into the tunnels, eyes peeled for movement. "Hello?" I call. "Giovanni?"

No one answers. But the air here feels different. Charged. I've never been the sort of person who believed in witchcraft and auras and all that hoo-ha shit, but I feel something in the tunnels down here. It's like the energy has shifted.

Someone else is here.

I blink into the darkness, willing my eyes to separate the shadows around me. I smell staleness in the air, and it reminds me of another person's breath.

"I know you're here." I don't shout this time. Instead, I speak in a low voice, to show whoever's hiding that I know she's close. Then, hoping I'm mistaken, I whisper, "Giovanni?"

"I'm not Giovanni."

The voice is closer than I expect, her breath a warm mist on my ear. She knocks into my shoulder, sending me slamming to the ground. Something blinks on above me: a flashlight.

"Boo," Elyse says, the light casting her face in an ugly yellow glow. The shadows stretch out her teeth, making them look long and pointed, leaving her eyes deeply hooded. I push myself back up to my feet, and Elyse smashes the flashlight across my face in a crack that sends stars bursting in front of my eyes. Pain flares through my skull, bright hot and burning.

The flashlight flickers but doesn't go out.

I throw my hands up over my head before Elyse can hit me again, and the flashlight slams into my arm, sending pain cracking from my elbow up through my shoulder. The jolt of it sends Elyse careening backward, about to lose her balance. With a scream I launch myself onto her, the two of us rolling to the ground in a mess of limbs and hair.

The flashlight rolls out of Elyse's fingers, coming to a stop beside the wall of skulls. The flickering light makes the jagged teeth and snarling mouths look like they're moving. They could be laughing.

Rage moves through me like an animal. Elyse didn't just torture me. She *enjoyed* herself. She liked causing another person pain. She's *sick*.

Suddenly my hands are claws, my fingernails digging into whatever I'm able to grasp. I feel Elyse's closed fist slam into the side of my face and hear something crack. The taste of copper fills my mouth. I hit back, and pain explodes through my fist as my fingers connect with the sharp bones in Elyse's cheek.

"*Vaffanculo!*" she shouts.

I find her shoulders and throw my weight into her, using the momentum to roll her onto her back. She's kicking beneath me, hands grasping, but I have the better angle and I'm able to keep her on the ground by sliding one leg over her chest. I dig my hands in her hair. Anger pumps through my veins, hot and seductive.

She grabs for my wrists, scratching the backs of my hands. I barely feel it.

"*Diavolina!*" she shouts. She spits, the saliva hitting me in the face, sliding down my cheeks. The anger inside burns brighter. I curl my fingers around her scalp, digging my fingernails into flesh.

The flashlight turns on and off from its spot a few feet

away, like a strobe light. It illuminates the wall of skulls. The packed-dirt floor. Elyse's terrified, blood-streaked face.

I pick her head up off the ground, fingers still curved around her skull, and slam it down again.

Elyse grunts. "Don't—"

I pick her head up. Slam it into the ground.

A flash of white light illuminates blood pooling in the dirt before suddenly switching off again. I slam her head into the ground again, and this time I feel something burst beneath my hands. Hot liquid coats my palms. Something warm and soft sticks to the pads of my fingers. It feels like peeled grapes.

The flashlight flickers on.

Elyse stares up at me, unblinking. Her eyes don't move. Her mouth is open, tongue sticking to her lower lip in a slick of blood. There's something on the ground beneath her, and at first I think we knocked one of the skulls off the wall while we were fighting. The sharp, white fragments on the ground look just like bone.

It is bone, I realize—*new* bone that's coated in blood and something pink and glistening that looks like . . .

My stomach churns. It's brain matter. I bashed Elyse's head in.

I have no memory of crawling off Elyse or stumbling away from her lifeless body. It's like my brain glitches, and then I'm wandering through the pitch-black tunnels—alone.

My calves ache. I feel like I've been walking for a very long time.

I make myself stop and lean against a wall to catch my breath. The wall is made up of smooth dirt—no skulls. Thank God. I look down at my hands, but they're practically invisible in the darkness. Just the outline of fingers.

Part of me doesn't want to believe that what happened with Elyse actually happened. It's been a long night. Maybe I imagined it. I clench and unclench my fingers, feeling for something sticky coating my skin. They feel dirty and grimy—but dry. I fold them together. They're trembling.

My brain skips again, and now the entrance to the catacombs yawns before me, the spiky black gate swinging in a light wind. The hinges creak as the gate blows open and then closed. The moon hangs in the sky beyond. Bright silver and peaceful.

I frown and look from side to side. I have no memory of finding the gate. No memory of moving away from the wall a few minutes ago.

*This is what going crazy feels like*, I think. The catacombs are messing with my mind, making me lose my grip on reality.

I close my eyes and flash on the cold, concrete walls of my room in solitary. All at once my lungs feel tight and hot. I can't breathe. I have to get out of here.

I lurch for the gate, certain Giovanni has already found his way out. He'll have the truck by now. I just want to leave this crazy village and never come back.

*"Bella!"*

The voice is desperate. A gasp in the darkness. I freeze, cold fear wrapping around my arms. I turn.

A narrow tunnel twists off to my left, and I never would have noticed it if Giovanni hadn't called out to me. He's lying across the ground, his face caved in and covered in a thick spray of blood. Francesca stands over him, a rock clasped in one hand.

She turns her head, slowly, to face me. Her lips split into a grin.

Giovanni gasps, blood spurting from between his teeth, *"Run."*

# CHAPTER 25

## *Before*

Therapy. Again.

It's my first day off meds, and everything feels fuzzy. The air around me has texture and weight. It presses against my eyelids and pushes my arms and legs down into the sofa. I feel like I'm sinking.

My nose twitches, but the idea of lifting my hand to scratch the itch seems exhausting.

I'm nestled into the corner of the couch, feet tucked beneath me, body curled around a fluffy pillow. I never get this comfortable at therapy, usually opting to perch right on the edge of the couch so that I can leap to my feet as soon as I'm dismissed. But the thought of holding my body upright seems impossible today.

I stare at a crack in the opposite wall instead, wondering what's beyond the broken space.

"Berkley."

I blink and drag my attention back to Dr. Andrews. Her face looks annoyed. Annoyed like *I've said your name at least a dozen times and you keep ignoring me.* Mara used to get like that, when she was studying, and it used to annoy me how I could say her name over and over again and she'd never hear me.

I swallow, and the saliva immediately disappears into the roof of my mouth and the backs of my teeth. Everything inside of me is tacky and dry.

"I'm sorry." I run my tongue along the insides of my cheeks, trying to draw moisture back into my mouth. "What did you say?"

Dr. Andrews presses her lips together. She says, "I asked you several times now if there was anything you wanted to discuss with me today."

Her expression is benignly interested, like always. She has her head tilted to the side, her eyes wide and eager, her mouth not quite smiling but pleasant. I wonder if they teach that look in shrink school. Or maybe Dr. Andrews practiced it herself, standing in front of her bathroom mirror, trying all the different smiles she could manage.

The thought makes me grin. *Poor Dr. Andrews.* Playing at being a therapist.

"You're smiling." Dr. Andrews leans forward in her seat, the pillows shifting behind her. "What are you thinking about right now?"

I consider telling her that I'm thinking about strangling her with my bare hands. But that would probably get me put back on the big-girl drugs. I move my eyes from the crack in the plaster to the clock above the door.

Time ticks past. *Tick. Tick. Tick.*

"Shall we talk about your friend? Tayla?"

I shrug with one arm.

*Tick. Tick. Tick.*

Dr. Andrews asks something else, but this time I don't even register her voice as words. I pull at a loose thread in the pillow, watching the two pieces of fabric slowly separate from one another and thinking that's exactly how I feel. Like I'm two pieces of fabric stitched together and every second I spend in this place is another second that my threads are being pulled away. My pillow is becoming unraveled.

"That's fine," Dr. Andrews says after a few more ticks. She closes her notebook with sudden finality. I lift my eyes without raising my head.

Have I worn her down? Have I won?

"Fine what?" My voice is muffled by the fabric of the pillow.

Dr. Andrews narrows her eyes, the skin at the corners

creasing. "If you don't want to talk, we'll have to find another way of treating you." She drums her fingers against the top of the notebook. "Perhaps more medication. You seemed to respond well to that."

I think of the last few days. Days spent in a drug-fueled fog, drooling on myself, barely strong enough to lift my head or brush my own hair.

"I'll get the prescription." Dr. Andrews half rises from her chair.

She's bluffing. Isn't she?

"Wait," I say.

Dr. Andrews pauses, and I can tell from her curled lips that I played right into her hand.

I swallow. My mouth is so dry that my tongue feels like it might split right down the middle. "What do you want me to say?"

Dr. Andrews lowers herself back to her chair. My eyes are closed, so I don't see her do it, but I hear the shuffling sound of fabric and pillows. "I just want the truth, Berkley. That's all I've ever wanted from you."

"The truth," I croak. My voice has no inflection. It sounds like something computer-generated and soulless. "Fine."

Dr. Andrews isn't smiling anymore. "Tell me why you feel responsible for Tayla's suicide."

I glance down at my lap, thinking about the party.

Lights strung up in Mara's living room. Punch bowl spiked with vodka. Me, Mara, and Harper getting ready in the bathroom, pregaming with a bottle of champagne. We didn't even invite Tayla to get ready with us. I don't think any of us expected her to come to the party at all.

Suddenly my hands are clenched, and they're trembling so badly that my knuckles are crunching against each other, pinching my skin. I unweave my fingers, press them flat against the tops of my thighs, but they don't stop shaking.

It's weird. Like my body is experiencing all the emotion I won't let myself feel.

"Right before she did it, she hooked up with this random guy at a party at our friend Mara's house," I say, still staring at my hands. My fingers are tapping now. Erratically jerking against my leg like they contain so much energy that they can't stay still. "She'd been dating the same guy forever, and it really seemed like they were in love. But we were about to leave for college, and I guess she just . . . freaked out or something. Anyway, she cheated on him."

I say all of this in a rush, without pausing to breathe or search for a word. The story just . . . slips out, like it's been there all along, waiting behind my teeth for me to set it free.

I press my hand flat against my leg. "Her boyfriend found out and dumped her. Our other friends stopped talking to her, too." I think of Mara and Harper turning their backs on Tayla in the cafeteria at school. Dropping their bags in the seat that used to be hers. Pretending they couldn't hear her when she tried to talk to us. "It was supposed to be, like, a punishment, sort of. It wasn't my idea to do that or anything, but I played along. We'd been friends since kindergarten, and I just stopped answering her texts. I'd walk past her in the hallway like she wasn't even there. I think . . . I think that's the reason she did it. Killed herself, I mean."

There's a beat of silence.

"Tell me about the night of your panic episode."

A tear slips down my cheek, and I brush it away with an angry flick of my hand. "I did some drugs with Harper and Mara, like I told you. Stupid stuff. Molly or whatever. I remember going into the bathroom to fix my lipstick, and when I looked in the mirror it was like . . ."

My voice dies in my throat. I close my eyes. Swallow.

"It was like I was looking at Tayla. Like she was looking out at me, through the mirror. She was mad at me because of what I did. I just sort of . . . snapped after that. Everything kind of . . . went black."

Dr. Andrews clears her throat. I look up in time to see her press her lips into a thin smile, blinking hard.

She seems to struggle to keep the shock and horror from her face.

"That's good work, Berkley," she says, and I guess I've been underestimating how good of a doctor she is, because her voice is serene, without a hint of the disgust she surely feels. She actually sounds like she believes what's she's saying. "You can go back to your room now."

# CHAPTER 26

*After*

The streets are practically empty, but I imagine I hear footsteps thudding behind me. *Chasing* me. I push myself faster, dragging my injured leg down narrow lanes and dark alleyways, over cool cobblestones.

The sun has only just begun to peek over the tops of crumbling buildings, casting everything around me in gold and shadow. A few stray partygoers stagger home from the festival. Some laugh and sway on too-high heels, voices sharp as broken glass. The rest gaze vaguely ahead, too wrecked to notice anyone outside of themselves.

Their presence calms me. I slow to a fast walk and

check over my shoulder, looking for Francesca's green-tinged hair in the shadows. But she hasn't caught up to me. *Yet.*

I keep expecting someone to stop me, ask me what happened. But I blend in. Just another wasted party girl coming back from the festival, covered in corn-syrup blood. No one gives me a second glance.

I release a dry sob when I finally reach the door to Mara and Harper's apartment. My entire body sags, collapsing against it. I've never been so relieved to see anything in my life.

I manage to gather enough energy to lift my arm and bang my fist against the wood. "Harper!" My voice is scratchy. Raw. "*Harper*, are you there? Please!"

There's a creak of floorboards behind me. I whirl around, heart pounding in my ears. But the stairwell stays empty.

I bang harder, using both fists now, fingers twitching. What if they aren't here? They freaked the last time I disappeared. What if they're out looking for me now?

My heart skips—

And then the door creaks open and Harper is standing in front of me, still wearing her devil's horns and teddy. Blinking.

"Berkley?" She pulls the door open wider, and I stumble inside, anxiously checking over my shoulder one last time. No Francesca.

Out of the corner of my eye, I notice Harper's head jerk up and down, taking in my ripped underwear, the mud, the blood. A shocked giggle bursts from her mouth.

"Looks like *you* had quite a night." Scandalized shake of her head and then, as though it's just occurring to her, "*Bad* girl. We were *so* worried. We looked everywhere for you."

Her voice is lilting, singsong. She's drunk. She spins in place, falling backward over the arm of the couch and landing on the cushions with another snort of giggles.

For a moment, I just stare at her. She stayed at the party. She and Mara took shots and grinded on strangers while I was stabbed and drowned and burned. They held hands and danced to Italian techno while I ran for my life, Giovanni's screams still echoing in my ears.

I should be angry. Furious. But the feeling that rises inside of me is something else:

*Jealousy.*

All I wanted was a normal summer. Not even a whole summer—a normal *two weeks*. Some girls get *everything*. Why couldn't I have this?

A tear hits my cheek, and I wipe it away, angry. There's no time to feel sorry for myself.

"Harper." I grab for her shoulder, but she squirms beneath my fingers, making a face.

"Fucking *ow*, Berk, that hurts!"

"You have to listen to me—"

A bleary Mara walks into the room, rubbing her eyes with a fist. She's already changed into an oversized NYU T-shirt, and the ragged hem hangs past her knees.

She's moaning, "Harper, I thought I told you—" And then her eyes land on me and widen. "Jesus! Where the hell have you been? We looked, like, everywhere on earth for you! You could have told us that you were going to run off with—"

She bites back the rest of that sentence, eyes flicking over the deep gash on my leg, the cuts hatched across my cheeks. Her expression twists. "Is that *real* blood?"

Harper blinks at us from the couch, her mouth going slack. She slurs, "How could that be real?"

"I don't have time to explain," I say in a rush. "We have to pack and . . . and someone should check flight times and . . ." I know I'm not making sense, but my breath is running wild, my heart vibrating in my ears. Everything inside of me is screaming *hurry.*

*Run. Move. Get out.*

I feel another jolt of disappointment for my lost summer in Italy, but there's no time for that now. I start moving toward the hall that leads to my room. "I need five minutes. You guys call a taxi."

Harper and Mara share a look they think I'm too stupid or too panicked to see.

"Are you guys even listening?" Cool anger surges

through me, making my fingers twitch. They had *all* summer here. What do they have to be pissed about? "We have to *go*."

"We don't understand, sweetie." Mara doesn't seem to know what to do with her face. She juts her chin out at a stubborn angle, mouth twitching in a strange half smile. "Why do we need to go? Who hurt you?"

She speaks in a little-kid voice that makes me want to slap her.

I force myself to breathe. "Something happened at the party last night."

Harper sits up too suddenly, knocking a pillow to the floor with her knee. I can see her mind working against the booze still dulling her edges. "Wait, did that Giovanni guy do this to you?"

"I'm calling the police," Mara says, ever practical. She already has her cell out, fingers tapping at the screen.

"No!" I grab it from her, but my hands are shaking and it slams to the floor, a crack spiderwebbing across its screen.

Mara scowls. "Damn it, Berk!"

"Giovanni didn't do anything." I press the heels of my hands into my eyes. That jealous feeling is coiling tighter, wrapping itself around my lungs. *All I wanted was to be normal.*

"Look," I try again, "there isn't time to explain right

now. We *have* to get out of here, okay? Can you *please* just trust me on this?"

"You said that already." Mara crosses her arms over her chest, her voice gone cold. "Berkley, you're not making sense."

"I *would* make sense if only . . ." A sob bubbles up my throat. *Normal*, I'm still thinking, desperate. I just wanted normal. Not epic. Not amazing, just *normal*.

How the *fuck* did it go so wrong?

Gasping, I try again. "I'm trying to make sense. I just need you to trust me . . ."

"Calm down, it's okay." Harper is suddenly in front of me. She runs the backs of her fingers along my arm, like she's calming a spooked dog. "Look, it's, like, five o'clock in the morning. There's no way there are any flights right now. Why don't you go take a shower and get changed and we'll sit down with some tea and talk this all over, okay? It'll give you a little time to sort things out in your head."

*Sort things out in your head.*

I feel a jolt slam through me. That means *I don't trust you*, clear as if she'd actually spoken the words out loud. It means *we think you imagined everything.*

It means *you're still crazy, bitch.*

Of course they would think that. I spent all night getting tortured, but *of course* they would assume I imagined it all. They have no idea what things have been like for me, not just for the past few days, but for the past year—for my whole life.

Life isn't fair. *Nothing* is fair.

I back the rest of the way down the hall, feeling for the door to my room behind my back. Harper's face closes off. She matches Mara's folded arms.

"You need help, Berkley," she says in a different tone of voice, the last of her drunkenness softening the edges of her words. "We both think so."

I release a hiss of breath through my teeth, like I've been hit. "I need to go *home*."

A wry laugh from Mara. "Yeah, I think we can all agree on that."

"Then *help* me!"

Harper says, "That's what we're trying to do."

"You aren't telling us what's going on," Mara adds.

"No, help me *go*. We should be packing. We should be—" Banging shudders through the apartment, cutting me off. I flinch and jerk my head around to stare at the door. My nerves flare. Someone's at the door.

Francesca.

# CHAPTER 27

Razor-edged silence stretches between the three of us. For a long moment, nobody speaks.

Then—

*Bang. Bang. Bang.* The door vibrates in its frame.

Dazed, Harper starts across the living room.

"Don't answer!" My voice sounds scraped raw. I tighten my fingers around the door to my room, and only then do I realize they're trembling. *"Please*, Harper."

Harper says, eyebrows shooting up, "Why wouldn't I answer?"

"Just trust me, okay? You have to—"

But she's already shaking her head. She pulls the

door open and says, to someone I can't see, *"Come posso aiutarla?"*

Muffled Italian answers back. Harper starts to respond, then makes a sound of surprise and takes a quick step back as a man in a stiff uniform shoves into the apartment. His belly strains against his polo, but his arms are thick and muscular. A shiny silver gun hangs from his waist.

My breath catches. Poliziotto.

I don't know whether to be relieved or terrified, so I shrink into the door to my bedroom, wishing I could disappear.

The poliziotto is sputtering in Italian, his words quick and hard to follow.

"I don't understand," Harper says, finally, in English. "A boy was . . . *ucciso*? Is that . . . killed?"

*Killed.* The word drops through me like a stone.

I don't realize I'm sinking until I feel the floor beneath my legs. My throat closes up, and every one of my muscles pulls tight, like they're attached to slowly winding screws.

Giovanni is dead.

The poliziotto drags a hand back through his dark hair, narrow eyes moving jerkily around the living room before landing on me. He taps his gun with his thumb and nods to someone I can't see. "This is her, no?"

There's a shift in the hall outside the door. A shadow stretches long across the floor, and then Francesca steps into the room.

Blood drips from a gash on her head, streaking her face with red and matting her green-and-black hair to her cheeks. Her dark, flat stare bores into me.

Mara subtly shifts her body in front of mine, one hand reaching for me. *Protecting* me. I wind my fingers through hers.

Whatever else has happened, Mara and Harper won't let anything hurt me. Right?

"I remember you. You work at the trattoria down the street, right?" Mara says. "What does she have to do with this?"

"This is my sister," the poliziotto answers. "She is the only witness to a crime she says your friend is involved in." To Francesca, softer, "Is this the girl who hurt you?"

At the sound of her brother's voice, Francesca changes. Her shoulders curve inward, fingers tangling in the hem of her bloody dress. She says, chin wobbling, *"Si, fratello.* Yes. This is her."

"What does that mean?" Mara's voice cracks. She squeezes my fingers so tightly the bones crunch together. "Berkley didn't kill anyone."

I hear a raw, choking sound from Harper.

"She's *lying,*" I say. "She kidnapped me from the festival—her and these two other girls. Elyse and—"

"Angelica." The poliziotto nods solemnly. "And Elyse. The other two victims, yes."

"Oh *God*." Harper presses a fist to her mouth and keels over, hair swinging forward to block her face. Mara drops my hand. My fingers feel suddenly cold.

"Three people?" she murmurs.

I feel a prickle move through the air. This is worse than knives and torture. Worse than drowning in an icy lake. Worse than losing Giovanni. This is *prison*. A small concrete cell with no windows and no chance of escape. My freedom—everything I've worked so hard for—gone.

Francesca tilts her head up, catching my eye. Her lip curls.

"She's lying!" I say again. No one seems to hear me. I reach for Mara's arm. "Mara, please—"

Mara shakes me off with a violent jerk. "I knew your story didn't make any sense." Her whole body is trembling now. "You've been getting worse every day. Oh *God*."

"You have to believe me!" I shoot Harper a ferocious stare. The air in the apartment feels bruised. "Harper, come on, you believe me, right?"

But Harper is shaking her head. She straightens, pushing her hair back, and I see that her cheeks are streaked with tears. "Didn't you hear what he said, Berkley? Three people are *dead*. How are we supposed to believe anything you say?"

"You will have to let me take her in now," the

poliziotto says. Francesca's mouth curves into a small, private smile.

"You bitch!" I lunge for her, but Mara's in front of me again, one arm holding me back. "She's smiling! Can't you see that? She's *enjoying* this."

"Berkley," Mara hisses through clenched teeth. "Stop, okay? Just stop."

And then she shifts to the side, no longer blocking the officer's path down the hall, and nods to him.

I freeze. "You're letting him take me?"

"You're still sick." Tears streak down Harper's cheeks. She sniffles and runs the back of her hand beneath her nose. "They never should have let you out of the institute."

"We're worried about you," Mara adds in a quiet voice.

"You think this happened because *I'm* sick?" I push my hair back over my shoulders so that everyone can get a clear view of my face. The burns climbing up my chin and over my eyebrows. The deep purple bruise blossoming over my forehead. "What do you think happened to me tonight?"

Harper and Mara glance at the poliziotto, saying nothing. As though on cue, he moves to the center of the room, putting his body between me and my friends. He's actually *protecting* them from me.

"You're making a mistake," I say. Rage moves through

me like an animal. *Cowards.* "You have no idea how bad things are about to get."

"Berkley—"

Fury radiates through my words, making them tremble. "But you *will*."

# CHAPTER 28
## *Before*

"**D**id you try the gray stuff?" Sofia asks.

I scuff the toe of my shoe over the concrete floor, sending a squeaking sound echoing down the hallway. From what I remember of the lunch we just ate, everything was kind of gray. "Which gray stuff?"

"I don't know what it was, but it was kind of . . . wobbly. Oatmeal, maybe?"

I purse my lips. I remember what she's talking about. It did sort of look like oatmeal, all gray and lumpy. Dad used to make me oatmeal every morning in the fall, only he'd add apples and cinnamon, brown sugar and walnuts. It tasted like pie when he was finished.

"Why would they serve oatmeal for lunch?" I ask, pushing the memory away. Just thinking about it makes my heart hurt.

Sofia shrugs. "Leftovers, probably."

We're making the way back to our dorm room. We only have an hour and a half to kill, and then it's back to the activity room for art therapy. I used to skip that sort of shit, back when I thought this was all a joke, but Sofia tells me it's good to be social. It shows the nurses that I'm "committed to my recovery." She says it'll help me get out of here faster.

We turn the corner to the hallway that leads to our room. My eyes pass unseeingly over the dark, narrow space before snagging on something unfamiliar—a person.

I stop short. Dr. Andrews is standing outside our door.

She looks up as Sofia and I shuffle toward her, shifting her ever-present clipboard so that it's in front of her chest. "Berkley! Good, I'm glad I caught you."

She pauses for a moment, like she's waiting for me to contribute something. I glance at Sofia, who shrugs.

"What are you doing here?" I blurt.

If my bluntness bugs Dr. Andrews, she doesn't show it. She smiles serenely, and her eyes shift from me to Sofia. "I was hoping we might speak in private?"

"Anything you have to say to me you can say in front of Sofia."

Dr. Andrews taps the edge of her clipboard with her pen. When she doesn't say anything for what feels like a full minute, I sigh, giving in.

"Do you mind?" I ask Sofia.

Sofia shakes her head, waiting in the hallway as I push open our door and step into the room. Dr. Andrews follows and carefully closes the door behind us.

"You two seem to be getting quite close." There's a carefulness to her voice that makes me wonder whether she thinks this is a good idea.

"Sofia was there for me when I needed her," I say.

Dr. Andrews taps her closed lips with the tip of her pen.

"You said you had something to talk to me about?" I ask.

"Oh, right. I just wanted to stop by to let you know that I feel like we made real progress yesterday. That was the first time you opened up to me about the problems you've been dealing with over the last year. I'm proud of you."

I frown, remembering the closed look on Dr. Andrews's face when she ended our last session. "I thought you were freaked out."

"Freaked out?" Her face breaks into a smile. "Berkley, no, of course not. It sounds like you've been dealing with a lot of pain, carrying the burden of your friend's suicide.

I'm really proud of your breakthrough. I've suggested that you continue with outpatient therapy twice a week, but otherwise I see no reason to keep you here."

The rest of her words turn to white noise. I look at her face and I see her lips moving, but her voice sounds mumbling and nonsensical.

"Stop," I choke out. "I'm sorry, are you saying that I can go home?"

A thin smile crosses her lips. "That's correct. Congratulations."

I can feel myself nodding, even as everything inside my head turns to static and buzzing. No more gray walls and faded blue T-shirts and Wite-Out manicures. No more lumpy mystery food and art therapy in the activity room. I'm going home.

I picture my bedroom, with its big bay windows and photo collage on the door. Movie nights with my parents every Friday. I used to think it was lame how they made us do weekly "family time," but now I find myself smiling just thinking about it. And my bed—oh God, how I've missed my bed! I have this amazing four-poster bed at home with a mattress so thick and fluffy you just sink into it, like a cloud. I have a closet filled with clothes and shoes. I have friends. Boyfriends. A whole life.

And I'm getting it all back.

I must do a pretty shitty job of holding in my

excitement, because Dr. Andrews actually laughs. The sound makes me flinch. I don't think I've ever heard her laugh before.

"I can see that you're looking forward to being rid of this place." She drops a hand on my shoulder and squeezes. "Go on and live your life."

I hear the door open and close behind me just a few seconds after Dr. Andrews leaves the room. There's a shuffling sound of footsteps.

"What's up with her?" Sofia asks.

"I'm going home." My voice is barely a whisper, not quite ready to believe what I'm saying.

"What?"

A smile cuts across my face. It stretches my lips so wide they actually hurt. I squeal and whirl around, throwing my arms around Sofia's neck. She's so surprised that she stumbles back a few steps, her arms hanging at her sides.

"I'm getting out!" I squeeze her shoulders. "They're finally letting me go!"

I pull away, breathless. The corners of Sofia's mouth twitch. Her eyes travel over my face, narrowing. "You told them the truth?"

"Of course," I say. "That's why they're letting me go. Dr. Andrews said I made 'progress,' can you believe it?"

Something dark flashes through Sofia's eyes. "You told the *whole* truth? You didn't leave anything out this time?"

"That's right." I open our closet and pull my suitcase off the top shelf, where it's started to gather dust. It's still mostly packed from last week. I only bothered taking out a few hair elastics and the stuffed hippo my mom made me bring.

I heave the suitcase onto my bed, knocking the hippo to the floor and making the mattress springs creak noisily.

I move to pick up the hippo, but Sofia stops me, one hand pressed to my shoulder. "Let me get this straight," she says softly. "You told Dr. Andrews that you *killed* someone, and she's still letting you out of here?"

Time slows down. I pick up the hippo without realizing what I'm doing and straighten back up, blinking. "What are you talking about?"

A muscle near Sofia's eye twitches. "The video, silly. Don't tell me you don't remember."

Something thick and heavy rises in my throat. She can't know about that.

I close my eyes, and it starts playing in my head, like it was cued.

It's jerky, the image dark. Someone took it from the hall—you can see the edge of the door. At first it's hard to tell what you're looking at—just two shapes fumbling in the darkness—and then the noises start.

A belt buckle clicks. Metal teeth scrape as jeans unzip. And then, a second later, moaning. Whoever's holding the phone giggles.

"Get closer," someone whispers off camera. The image zooms in shakily.

The guy stays in shadow, but the light from the hall catches Tayla's parted lips, her sweaty hair. She sits up, flashing her boobs at the camera. That's where the video clicks off abruptly, like whoever was filming lost her nerve.

By the next day, every single person in our school had seen it.

I try to keep my voice steady, but a tremor creeps in. "How do you know about that?"

Sofia tilts her head at a dangerous angle. "It's lucky I found you, you know? I thought I might be stuck in here forever."

I set the stuffed hippo back onto my bed, backing away from her. "What're you talking about? You're freaking me out."

Sofia moves toward me slowly, her toes curling into the dirty concrete. "Don't freak out. You're going to help me. Well, we're going to help each other. But first you have to admit your sin."

My back hits the wall. "What the fuck?"

"Tell the truth, Berkley. What happened to Tayla?"

My jaw tightens. "She committed suicide."

"Why?"

Sweat gathers in my palms. "She . . . she was upset because someone took a video of her cheating on her boyfriend," I stutter. "It was an *accident*."

"It didn't look like an accident to me."

"How the fuck would you know?" I snap. Angry tears gather in the corners of my eyes. I blink them away.

"I know a lot of things about you," Sofia says.

I grab her by the shoulders and shove her away from me. She starts laughing. Actually *laughing*. Like this is all some big joke.

It's the laughter that does it. Something inside of me loosens, the final thread pulling free. My knees feel watery. I sink to the floor, my hands falling limp at my sides.

*She knows*, I think. I try to inhale, but my breath catches and an ugly sob rips up my throat. The tears keep coming. They fall over my cheeks, dripping from my chin. *Oh God*, I think. *Oh God . . .*

Through her laughter, Sofia chokes out, "Tell the truth, and this will all be over."

I'm shaking my head back and forth, back and forth. I can't tell the truth. I *can't*.

Sofia says, "You'll finally be free. We'll both be free."

"What do you—"

"Tell me!" Sofia screams.

*"Fine!"* My voice sounds too high, a hiss of breath

between clenched teeth. I lower my head to my hands, digging my fingers into my hair, struggling to inhale. "I . . . I took the video, okay? I shot it on my camera phone, but only because Harper and Mara *made* me. They were there with me, and they told me that I had to record it or I wouldn't be able to sit with them at lunch anymore. They said Tayla deserved it, because she was always acting all perfect even though she clearly wasn't. It was, like, a joke. Nobody was supposed to see it!"

My throat closes, making it impossible to speak. I gasp for air, but I can't seem to get it into my lungs. My chest feels tight, like I'm back in solitary, a thick strip of canvas strapping me down. I grasp at my chest, like I'm trying to pull the bindings away, but my fingers close around nothing.

"I'm a little disappointed, Berkley," Sofia says, too calm. "I gave you every chance to come clean, to admit your sin, and you're still hiding behind these bullshit excuses."

"Tayla and I were friends," I say. I think of how Tayla and I used to build forts out of the sofa cushions when we were kids. How we borrowed each other's clothes so often I could never remember which tops were hers and which were mine. "If I'd known what she'd . . . I wouldn't have . . . I'd *never* have . . . I didn't mean to kill her."

Sofia rips the fitted sheet off her mattress and starts twisting it between her fingers. "Good, Berkley. Very good."

Tears cling to my eyelashes, making everything blurry. "What?"

Sofia ignores me. She crosses the room, yanking the sheet off my mattress, too. Her movements are jerky, almost mechanical. She ties the sheets together.

"What are you doing?" I ask. "Are you going to hurt me?"

"Don't worry. We don't hurt our own."

Sofia climbs onto her bed. She tosses one end of the sheet-rope around the pipe jutting across our ceiling. I watch her fingers tighten, testing the knot. I can't look away.

Once it's secured, she gathers the other end in her hands and ties a loop.

All the hair on the back of my neck stands straight up. I push myself to my feet. "Sofia—"

But she's too quick. She has the noose around her neck before I can reach for her. She steps off the edge of the bed—

The rope pulls tight. Sofia's neck snaps, and her head drops forward, chin smacking into her chest. Her arm twitches—muscle failure. I ball a hand near my mouth, fighting back a scream.

Then she goes still, her body swaying in small circles. The only sound in the room is the fabric groaning beneath her weight.

I don't have to press my fingers to her neck to know that I'm not going to find a pulse. Her skin has already taken on a pale cast, like spoiled meat, and thin, blue veins are crawling up her neck and cheeks. Her eyes bulge from their sockets, the whites already turning bloody. The sheet-rope digs into the skin on her neck, making her head look puffy, like a balloon about to burst.

I take a step closer, lowering a trembling hand from my mouth. "Sofia—"

Her head jerks up. Her eyes are burning red, lit from some fire within. The sound of my scream echoes in the small room.

Her mouth falls open, and black smoke pours out. It seeps in through my nose and mouth and eyes. It feels . . . dark. Heavy. Like something unfurling inside me.

Something that burns.

I swat at the smoke, but it keeps coming. I try to scream, "You crazy bitch . . . get off of me . . ."

Sofia's dead body smiles. Her voice echoes through the room.

"Hold still."

# CHAPTER 29

*After*

The poliziotto pulls his gun out of its holster. "Miss, I will need you to come with—"

I feel my strength return to me, and I grab him by his wrist. My fingers curl around skin and bone, tightening until I hear something *crack*. The sound echoes through the room. His hand flops to the side.

"*Troia*," he chokes out. His fingers are still curled around the gun, but his wrist is broken and he can't hold it straight. *Pity.* He falls to his knees, horror etched across his face. "*Diavolina* . . . what did you do?"

I should let go. Surely he's learned his lesson by now. But there's something inside me that can't do that. It's a sick, hungry feeling, and the more I lean into it, the more it seeps into me, stretching through my arms and legs and into my fingers, my toes, my brain.

He deserves this. He deserves everything I do to him. He's hurt people, I know it.

I twist, relishing how flimsy this big, strong man's wrist feels beneath my fingers. Harper and Mara have started shouting. I'm vaguely aware of Francesca pulling at my arm, nails digging into my skin, screaming.

I keep twisting until the poliziotto's hand is folded back against his wrist, his knuckles brushing the top of his arm, fingers stretched up toward his elbow. Bones snap and rip through skin, the jagged white shards glistening with blood and sinew.

The gun drops to the floor. The thud of metal hitting wood sounds strangely heavy. I toss the hand away.

Harper shrieks and stumbles backward as the hand slides toward her feet, fingers still twitching, blood streaking along the floor behind it. Mara doesn't move. She looks paralyzed. The poliziotto drops to the floor, sobbing.

Francesca lunges for me, her eyes like lit coals. She steps into the pool of her brother's blood, and her foot slides out from beneath her, sending her crashing to the floor. She grabs for me as she falls, tangling her fingers in my hair, and I go down with her.

We're a mess of arms and legs. Blood coats our skin.

Francesca's skin is slick and wet. She's hard to hold on to. She wrestles me to the ground and slides one leg across my chest to straddle me. She holds me down by the shoulders.

"You are evil!" Spit flies from her lips. "Look what you did!"

I squirm, tugging one arm free. There's not much I can do to her from this position on the ground, so I grasp desperately for anything I can sink my fingers into. I manage to catch the edge of her cheek, my thumb hooking into her eye socket.

Her face goes slack with fear. She tries to pull away, but I hold fast, digging my thumb into the soft tissue of her eye. It gives easily, like a grape. I hear a squelching *pop*, and then blood is pouring down her face. She jerks backward, falling to the ground with a thud that sends her head whacking into the floor.

She's still screaming, but no words come out. The sound isn't human. She clutches for her face.

I lean over and grab the gun from the floor, aiming for her chest. Calmly, almost lazily, I pull the trigger. The firecracker *pop* of a gunshot explodes through the room. Francesca collapses to the ground, her body seizing before going completely still.

The poliziotto is screaming now. "Please. I am begging you . . . please . . . stop . . . I have a family . . . children . . ."

"Stop!" Harper shrieks. "Please, Berkley, just stop."

Mara's face has gone white. She keeps shaking her head, her eyes unfocused. "Oh God," she murmurs. I don't know if she realizes she's speaking. "Oh God . . . oh God . . . oh God . . ."

They're acting like I just killed some beloved pet and not the girl who tortured me for hours.

"You're sick," Harper sobs. "Please . . . you're sick!"

"I've told you a thousand times"—I aim the gun at the poliziotto—"I'm *fine*."

I pull the trigger, releasing another *pop*. The poliziotto's eyes go dim. He stumbles backward, then falls to the floor as blood blossoms across his chest and spreads, seeping into the cracks and crevices in the floorboards. Already, it's starting to smell.

People don't realize how much blood reeks, how it has this sharp copper and meat scent. When there's enough of the stuff, the smell hangs in the air like fog. It clings to the inside of your lungs when you breathe it in.

I wrinkle my nose as the blood creeps under my toes, all sticky and warm. I tilt my head to the side, examining the dead man's face. Eyes look so different when there's no life behind them.

"You . . . you killed them," Mara whispers. It isn't until she speaks that I realize she and Harper have finally stopped screaming. "How could you do that?"

I lift my face, catching her eye. My veins burn hot beneath my skin, liquid fire running through my body. Mara flinches and looks away from me.

I say, "Your hands aren't exactly clean."

The girls go still. There's something in the air between us now: the heavy weight of a secret.

"What are you talking about?" Mara whispers.

"You haven't forgotten about Tayla already, have you?" I ask.

Harper says, under her breath, "We *promised* we'd never talk about that!"

Of course they did.

"No," I say. "The two of you made *Berkley* promise. Remember? You knew she felt shitty about what happened, so you said that if she told anyone what you all did to Tayla, you'd ruin her. That's how you put it: *ruin*."

Harper's voice rises a few octaves. "Why are you talking like that? *You're* Berkley."

"God, you're easy to fool. I'm not Berkley, but I know the truth." I lift my foot, drawing circles in the blood with my big toe. "You dared Berkley to take that video of Tayla, and then you made sure everyone in school saw it."

"What do you mean you're not Berkley?" Mara says, her voice panicky.

"Trying to change the subject, Mara? Can't you stand hearing about your crime? Tayla lost her boyfriend and her place at school because of that video. All her friends stopped talking to her. And then she killed herself. All because of your funny little joke."

Harper is suddenly between us, baring her teeth, her fear giving way to fury. "No one *made* you do anything. You're just as responsible for Tayla as the rest of us."

She doesn't get it. Neither of them do. They still think this is about Tayla and Berkley. They still think they can walk away.

"All I wanted was another chance to live my life. To be normal." I twirl the gun around my finger like it's a toy, and Harper stumbles away from me, swearing. "My whole life, I lived by the rules, and look where it got me. All my friends betrayed me. My boyfriend turned his back on me. My mother died . . ."

"Your mother's not dead," Mara mutters. "Why—"

She trails off, her eyes widening in horror as my face starts to change. The bones shifting and morphing beneath my skin is a weird sensation—a wrongness, but not painful. Something warm rises inside my chest, and I inhale, lifting my face to the ceiling as I allow it to overtake me. When I lower my face again, I catch sight of my reflection staring back at me from the mirror on the wall.

My *real* reflection.

"You're not Berkley," Mara whispers.

"You're that girl," Harper chokes out. "That crazy girl in the hospital."

*Crazy girl.* Fury pulses through me like a second heartbeat.

"My name is Sofia." I step over the dead poliziotto, trailing bloody footprints behind me. "Or didn't Berkley ever tell you?"

Harper and Mara don't answer. They grasp for each other, fingers intertwining as they inch toward the door behind them.

"Berkley didn't deserve her perfect life," I say. "But at least she felt some remorse for what she did. You bitches don't even care. You're partying in Italy like you didn't slut-shame a girl into committing suicide last year."

"Berkley told you?" Mara whispers, horrified.

"No one had to tell me anything," I say. "The devil always knows a sinner."

Harper reaches behind her back, fingers curling around the doorknob. She turns it. But it doesn't budge.

"I'm going to enjoy killing you," I say.

Harper is the first to run. She pushes off the door and darts into the kitchen, yanking open a drawer beneath the sink. The clanking of metal tells me she's looking for a weapon.

I close my eyes, letting the heat overtake me. It stretches through my arms and legs. It curls into my toes and fingers. I open my eyes again, and they feel like lit matches.

Something starts to hiss. Harper freezes, one hand still

poised above the open drawer, fingers twitching. Slowly, she turns toward the sink . . .

A dozen poison-green snakes crawl up from the drain, hissing and wriggling over each other in a tangled mess of muscle and scales.

Their pink tongues dart out from their tiny black mouths. Their beady eyes reflect Harper's horror back at her.

She stumbles backward, kitchen utensils clattering to the floor around her. She screams.

The snakes quickly fill the sink. They slide over the edge and tumble onto the floor. They're too knotted together to separate from one another. They slither toward Harper in a single grotesque unit. She races out of the kitchen, pushing past me to get to the apartment door. She curls both hands around the knob and pulls desperately.

"Let me out of here, you bitch!" she shrieks.

A snake pokes its head beneath the crack in the door. Harper spots it and jerks backward, screaming. Another follows, and another, until the snakes pour in from every crack and crevice, the sound of their hissing like white noise.

Harper's screams echo around us.

Mara doesn't think I'm watching her. She's been edging toward her room at the back of the apartment, slowly at first and faster now that she thinks I'm distracted. I watch her from the corner of my eye, relishing the look of relief that covers her face when she makes it to the hallway.

I crack my neck to the left and then to the right, the sound of popping joints drowned out by the hissing snakes. As though on cue, the glass in every framed picture in the apartment shatters, filling the air with razor-thin, cutting shards.

The glass pricks Mara's arms and face, leaving long, thin red lines along her perfect porcelain skin. She screams and covers her face, but the glass slices into the backs of her hands. She's crying now, thick baby tears that leave her gasping and snotting. Blood pours down her arms.

Harper has kicked most of the snakes away, squealing each time her foot comes into contact with scales. She tries the doorknob again, and this time it opens easily.

"Do you know how they get rid of demons here, Harper?" I snap my fingers, and Harper's teddy bursts into flame. "They *burn* them."

Harper swats at herself with both hands desperately, her eyes reflecting the flickering red of the fire. The fabric melts into her body, making her skin bubble and blacken. She drops to her knees.

I crouch in front of her, snakes slithering around my

legs. I feel the heat behind my eyes, and I know they're glowing bright red.

"You deserve this." I lift a hand to Harper's cheek. Her skin is cool to the touch, even as fire dances up her hair. "You killed a girl, and you felt no guilt. You refused to confess. Now it's your turn to die."

"No." Harper starts to sob, her tears reflecting the red-orange flames dancing in her hair. "Please. I'm sorry. I'm so sorry."

"I was friends with mean girls once," I tell her, standing. "Things didn't end well for them either."

Harper collapses to all fours, smoke quickly overtaking her. The fire burns the skin from her bones, eating away at her hair and her pajamas and her once beautiful face. After a few moments, all that's left is the charred, black husk of who she once was.

Which leaves Mara.

Mara is trying to crawl away, but there's too much blood. It coats her palms and pools on the floor. Every time she inches a hand forward, it slips out from beneath her, sending her face slamming into the floor.

"Poor Mara." I step over the bodies to reach her, walking slowly so she'll think she still has a shot at escaping. Her sobbing inches up a notch, and her hands have started to tremble. She clumsily pushes herself back on all fours and struggles to move forward.

"Did you really think you could kill a girl and there wouldn't be any consequences?" I ask, kneeling beside her. "I thought you were supposed to be the smart one."

Mara collapses onto the floor, a bloody heap of skin and hair. She covers her head with both hands.

"Please," she begs. "I didn't know. I didn't . . ."

"You didn't know that taking a sex tape of Tayla would convince her to slit her own wrists?"

"I'm sorry," Mara says. She's cradling her face in her hands. "So sorry. So, so sorry."

I wag my finger at her. "You're not actually sorry."

"Please . . . don't . . ."

"But that's why I'm here." I snap my fingers, and the knife Harper pulled from the kitchen flies across the room, embedding itself in Mara's back. She releases a wet, muffled gasp and collapses on the floor. "To make sure you die sorry."

Mara opens and closes her mouth a few times, her eyes clouding. A bubble of blood forms on her lips and then pops, speckling her face with red. The light in her eyes dies.

The heat bubbles up inside of me, hotter and hotter, until it's all that I can feel. My fingers twitch, and my lungs grow hot—they're practically boiling. I stand, stretching my arms out to either side.

It's happening.

Flames erupt from my fingertips. Little orange flowers licking at my nails. They travel through my fingers and over my wrists, carving lines up my arms. When they reach my head, they pour out of my eye sockets and nostrils and mouth.

The flames feel good. Like I'm being cleansed from the inside out.

Like redemption.

The fire leaps from my body to the thick rugs covering the wood floors. It crawls up the sides of the furniture and curls into the art hanging on the walls. It eats away wood and fabric and curtains and carpets. The apartment fills with roiling black smoke.

I start to laugh. The laughter is like medicine, ripping through me, tearing away all that is sinful and making me whole. This is a good death. A clean death. This is nothing to be ashamed of.

I'm still laughing as the smoldering building comes down around me.

# EPILOGUE

The coffin blends in with the cool gray sky. Raindrops glimmer from its steel-colored surface, and drizzle blurs the air above it, making a hazy rainbow that looks out of place in the sea of crumbling gravestones. The air is thick with the smell of dead flowers.

There's no crowd gathered around the coffin, no mourning family or teary-eyed friends. The only person in attendance is an ancient woman in a wheelchair. Her eyes are unfocused, and a blanket covers her shriveled legs, but she sits upright, spine ramrod-straight. Her face looks like a melting candle. Skin drips from her bones, pulling her cheeks so low that the blood-red insides of her eyelids roll open.

There's no priest. There wouldn't be, for a suicide, but the woman clenches a rosary anyway. She moves the beads between gnarled fingers. Half her mouth twists in a frozen snarl. The other half moves quietly, whispering.

Wind weaves between the gravestones, lifting the edge of the woman's blanket and rustling tufts of dandelion-fuzz hair. It carries her voice through the trees.

"... *diablo* ... *diablo* ..."

The sound of wood clicking against wood follows a moment later. If the woman notices the wind, she doesn't show it. She stares straight ahead. It's unclear how well she sees through those milky eyes. Unclear whether she notices anyone standing in the trees just a few feet from her. She doesn't look away from the coffin.

A cicada crawls up the side of the glossy gray wood, wings twitching. The woman's eyes fix on the insect, and the half of her mouth that's been whispering—the good half—twists, so that both sides of her lips match. Her face crumples, eyes disappearing in a mess of wrinkles, and she tries to stand. Her legs shake. She stumbles forward, one hand grasping for the side of the wheelchair.

"Diablo!" she screams. She's crying now, shoulders shaking and fat tears running down her cheeks. She throws the rosary beads at the coffin. "Diablo!"

She crosses herself and then drops back into the wheelchair, head turned like she can't stand to look at the coffin any longer. She braces her hands against the chair's wheels, but they're stuck in the mud and it takes her a few tries to get them rolling. I watch her weave down the path. And then she's gone.

The cicada leaps from the side of the coffin and lands on a tree a few feet away, wings trembling. I shoo it away.

I step out from behind my tree and make my way around the gravestones, mud squelching beneath my shoes.

The gravedigger looks up as I approach. His jumpsuit is already smudged with mud, grass shavings clinging to his thick-soled boots. He swipes a bandana across his forehead and then jabs his thumb at a button beside the coffin. A grinding noise fills the air as the great gray box sinks into the ground.

He jerks his chin at the coffin. "Such a shame when they're young like that," he says, shaking his head. He presses the bandana to his mouth.

"Shame," I agree, sweeping my long, dark hair over one shoulder. Wind whips at my dress, sending it flapping against the backs of my legs. My umbrella hasn't done much good. It's barely raining, but my black tights are already damp from the knees down.

"You gotta be cold," the gravedigger says, jabbing a shovel into the mound of dirt beside the coffin. Grunting, he drops it into the hole. "You ought to head inside. Nothing more to see out here."

"I don't really get cold." I kneel, careful to keep the edge of my dress from falling in the mud. The rosary beads look like bright red berries against the grass and dirt. I scoop them up, and the wood clicks together softly.

"You knew her, then?" The gravedigger squints, reading the name etched into the tombstone. "This . . . Sofia Flores?"

I stand, slipping the beads into my pocket. They're still wet, and they soak through the thin fabric of my dress, chilling the skin at my hip.

"I knew her well. I hope she's at peace now." The corner of my lip twitches. "She was a very sick girl."

The gravedigger gives me a look and then goes back to shoveling dirt onto Sofia's coffin, muttering something under his breath about crazy teenage girls. I smile at his back, lips pulled too tightly over my teeth. And then I turn and walk away, shaking off the cicada that has landed on my shoe.

It's chilly out, but I can feel heat building inside me. It licks my skin, growing hotter with each step I take, yearning for a new sinner to play with. There's always a new sinner, another sick girl with a secret waiting for me to show her who she really is.

I just have to find her.

# Acknowledgments

I've been writing the Merciless books for a long time, now, and I'm so lucky to have a truly brilliant team behind me making sure they end as strongly as they began. Thanks, again, to my wonderful Alloy family—specifically Hayley Wagreich, Josh Bank, and Sara Shandler. You are brilliant humans.

Thanks times about a million to my team at Razorbill. I couldn't have written this book without Jessica Almon to help me get it started and Jessica Harriton to help me bring it home. As always, I owe Casey McIntyre for about a million tiny things, from making sure I have coffee at events, to endless hours booking travel, to pre-panel pep talks. Thank you, thank you, thank you.

And, of course, Ben Schrank, Elora Sullivan, Felicity Vallence, Maria Fazio, and the rest of Razorbill's sales, marketing, and publicity team. I'm continually blown away by how hard you work to help people find my books.

In addition to the people named here, there are so many others working behind the scenes to make this book happen. I am grateful to all of you. I couldn't have done it without your support.

And finally, thanks to my fabulous, supportive family and friends. I'm consistently blown away by all of you.